The Twelve Days of Catmas

Kysa Steele

The Twelve Days of Catmas

Copyright © 2025 by Kysa Steele

Kysa Steele

1st edition: 2025
ISBN: 979-8-9989422-7-3 Paperback
ISBN: 979-8-9989422-8-0 Hardback
ISBN: 978-1-971434-10-0 Mas Market Paperback

KRAMPUS'S ROUTINE

Krampus had been doing this job for five hundred and thirty-seven years, four months, and sixteen days. Not that anyone was counting.

He was counting.

The morning routine never changed. Wake at 5 AM (he didn't need an alarm anymore; his body had calcified into punctuality). Black coffee, no sugar. Review the naughty list. Update the filing system. Sharpen the chains. Oil the bells. Prepare for another year of being fundamentally misunderstood by an increasingly entitled mortal population who seemed to think "consequences" were a suggestion rather than a cosmic law.

His lair reflected this philosophy: functional, efficient, stripped to essentials.

The stone walls were bare except for a single calendar—provided by Holiday HR, naturally—marking off the days until the season officially began. The hooks where tapestries once hung stood empty. The mantle held nothing but dust. In the corner, a second chair sat untouched, its

"

cushion still perfectly aligned from the last time he'd straightened it. Three years ago? Four?

The filing system took up the entire eastern wall: floor-to-ceiling cabinets organized by region, severity, and repeat-offense status. Color-coded labels in his own meticulous handwriting. Cross-referenced indices. A master spreadsheet updated daily. He'd even implemented a tracking system for behavioral patterns, correlating geographical data with socioeconomic factors to optimize his routes.

Last quarter's review, he presented the system to Santa. Seventeen slides. Data visualizations. Projected efficiency gains of 23%.

Santa had grunted. "Efficiency isn't everything."

The elves had exchanged glances when Krampus walked past their break room. One had whispered "obsessive" under his breath, not quite quietly enough.

Krampus stood before the filing cabinets now, updating a particularly egregious case from Stuttgart. It's the third year in a row. The child had graduated from petty theft to orchestrating an elaborate cryptocurrency scheme targeting elderly relatives. Impressive, in a bleak sort of way.

He filed the report under "Repeat Offenders: White Collar (Junior Division)" and closed the drawer with a satisfying *click*.

Silence.

His own breathing. The drip of water

somewhere in the stone depths. The slight creak as the building settled.

He poured a second cup of coffee. Realized he'd been standing alone in his kitchen for three minutes, staring at nothing. Set the cup down without drinking.

Partnerships were more trouble than they were worth. He'd learned that. Connection meant vulnerability. Caring about anything beyond work itself was a liability he could no longer afford.

The last time he'd taken a vacation—*one week*, that's all he asked for—the Black Plague happened.

HR wouldn't let him forget it.

There'd been a formal inquiry. A performance review. He'd stood alone before the Tribunal while Santa sent a memo—a *memo*—expressing "concern about operational gaps during critical periods." Not support. Not defense. Corporate-speak delivered by courier while Krampus faced the Board alone. A strongly worded memo about "the critical importance of continuous supernatural oversight during times of moral uncertainty." As if *he'd* personally released the rats. Santa hadn't said it, but Krampus saw it in his eyes after—the first flicker of doubt, the moment partnership became liability. The inquiries and performance reviews that followed were just bureaucratic echoes of trust already broken. As if wanting a single break after three hundred years of uninterrupted service was somehow irresponsible.

He hadn't asked for time off since.

Krampus moved to his desk—a massive slab of black oak that had witnessed the signing of at least three morally questionable treaties—and began the day's correspondence. Complaint forms, mostly. Someone in Bavaria objects to the psychological impact of his visit. Someone in Quebec claimed he'd traumatized their child by accurately describing the consequences of habitual dishonesty.

He responded to each with the same template:

Your feedback has been noted. Behavioral correction protocols remain in effect.
Regards,
Krampus.

Copy. Paste. Send. Copy. Paste. Send.

The morning stretched on.

At some point, he stood to retrieve a reference document from the lower cabinet, the one he never opened, the one that housed outdated materials from previous centuries, back when the operation had looked... different.

His hand hesitated on the drawer pull.

Don't.

But he was already opening it, already reaching past the obsolete record books and discontinued disciplinary guides, already finding the small wooden box wedged in the back corner.

Inside: a single ornament.

Hand-carved. Painted in colors that had faded to ghosts of themselves. Two initials intertwined in a design that had once meant partnership, teamwork, shared purpose.

K & S.

Someone had made it for them centuries ago. Before the work became mechanical. Before efficiency replaced meaning. Before Krampus decided that caring about anything was the fastest route to disappointment.

He stared at it for exactly five seconds.

Then he closed the box, shut the drawer, and returned to his desk.

Work. He always had work.

He told himself that was exactly how he wanted it. Had been telling himself that for five hundred and thirty-seven years.

The coffee had gone cold.

He drank it anyway.

Chapter One

THE MANDATE

The notification arrived at precisely 9:00 AM, because of course it did. Holiday HR had adopted "core business hours" three years ago, along with mandatory email signatures, an updated mission statement, and a truly baffling commitment to "leveraging seasonal synergies across all departmental touchpoints."

Krampus hated every word of that sentence.

The alert manifested as a glowing red envelope that materialized directly in front of his face, hovering at eye level with the aggressive cheerfulness of someone about to ruin your entire day.

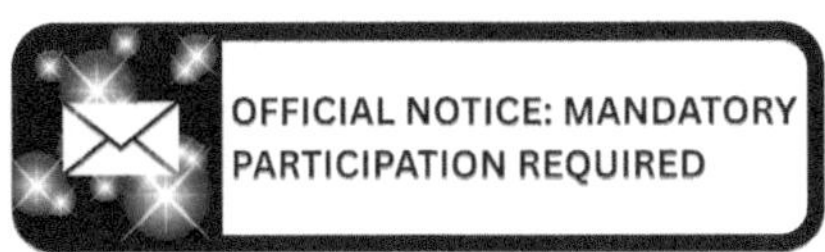

He glared at it.

It sparkled.

With a growl that would have sent mortals

running for consecrated ground, Krampus snatched the envelope from the air and tore it open.

***

FROM: North Pole Human Resources Department
TO: Krampus (Employee ID: KRM-1487-DISC)
RE: Mandatory Goodwill Outreach Initiative - PARTICIPATION REQUIRED

Dear Valued Seasonal Operations Partner,

As part of our ongoing commitment to fostering cross-departmental collaboration and promoting a culture of inclusive holiday cheer, you are hereby required to participate in this year's Goodwill Outreach Initiative.

This program is designed to strengthen interpersonal bonds between traditionally oppositional seasonal roles and create opportunities for professional growth through cooperative engagement.

***

Krampus stopped reading.

Then, against his better judgment, he kept reading.

***

Your participation is non-negotiable as per Section 47, Subsection 12(c) of the Unified Holiday Operational Charter, which states: "All entities engaged in behavioral correction protocols must demonstrate measurable commitment to positive relationship-building activities when directed by senior management."

Failure to participate may result in:
Please complete the attached compliance training module ("Fostering Cross-Departmental Seasonal Synergy: A 37-Slide Journey Toward Collaborative Excellence") within 48 hours.

We appreciate your cooperation and look forward to your enthusiastic participation!

Warmest Regards,

Tinsel Brightholly
Director of Workforce Optimization & Seasonal Morale
North Pole HR Department

Krampus stared at the letter. Then he read it again, certain he had hallucinated at least part of it.

No. It was real. All of it.

"*Enthusiastic participation,*" he muttered,

crumpling the letter in one clawed fist. "They want *enthusiasm.*"

A second notification popped up:

He clicked. He immediately regretted it.

The module opened in a shimmering window of aggressive pastels. Slide One featured an illustration of Santa and an elf high-fiving beneath a rainbow, accompanied by text in a font that could only be described as "aggressively whimsical."

FOSTERING CROSS-DEPARTMENTAL SEASONAL SYNERGY

Module 1 of 37

Learning Objective: Understanding the value of collaborative partnerships in a modern holiday framework

Krampus closed his eyes. Breathed deeply. Opened them again. The slide was still there.

Slide Two: *What is synergy? Synergy is when magical beings work together to create outcomes greater than the sum of their individual efforts!*

Slide Three: *Historical case study: Remember when Rudolph and Blitzen had that conflict over sleigh positioning? Communication solved everything!*

Slide Four began an extended metaphor involving gingerbread houses and "building foundations of trust."

Krampus made it to Slide Twelve before his clawed finger hovered over the window's close button.

"No," he said aloud. The words echoed off the stone walls, came back to him. "Absolutely not."

He navigated back to the original email and hit REPLY with more force than strictly necessary.

❋ ❋ ❋ ❋

TO: North Pole HR Department
FROM: Krampus
RE: RE: Mandatory Goodwill Outreach Initiative

No.

❋ ❋ ❋ ❋

He clicked SEND.
Satisfaction bloomed in his chest. Four seconds later, it died.

AUTOMATIC REPLY:
Thank you for your response! Unfortunately,

declination of mandatory programs is not permitted under current Holiday Operational Guidelines. Please refer to your employee handbook, Chapter 8: "When 'No' Means 'Yes, But with Extra Paperwork.'"

A new document appeared: seventeen pages of single-spaced legalese outlining the exact mechanisms by which he was, in fact, completely trapped.

There it was. Section 47, Subsection 12(c), Addendum VII, Clause 19.

Refusal to participate in mandated collaborative initiatives constitutes breach of operational contract and may result in immediate suspension of all seasonal privileges, including but not limited to: access to the naughty list, use of dimensional travel portals, and authorization to conduct behavioral interventions.

In other words: they could shut him down completely.

Krampus sat back in his chair. The leather creaked. He stared at the ceiling, counting the cracks in the stone he had memorized decades ago.

"This is corporate nonsense," he growled to the empty room. "Soul-crushing, performative, meaningless corporate nonsense."

Santa had gone soft. That was the problem.

All this talk of "positive engagement" and "building bridges" and "fostering understanding"—as if morality was something you could workshop into existence. As if discipline did not *require* someone willing to be the bad guy.

They used to understand that. *He* and Santa used to understand that.

Once upon a time, they worked together. A unified system: reward and consequence, light and shadow, hope and accountability. Two sides of the same operation, balanced and effective.

But that was before Santa decided that image mattered more than function. Before the rebrand. Before Holiday HR and their endless initiatives and their mission statements and their mandatory training modules about synergy.

Krampus pulled up the email again, scanning for loopholes. He found none.

There were always clauses. Legal traps embedded in cheerful language, ensuring compliance through the threat of professional annihilation.

He could fight it. Escalate to the Holiday Tribunal. Spend the next six months buried in arbitration hearings while his entire operation ground to a halt.

Or he could comply.

Complete whatever performative nonsense they had planned, suffer through it with his dignity barely intact, and return to his work.

The choice was not really a choice.

"Fine," Krampus muttered, pulling up the training module again. "Thirty-seven slides. I've endured worse."

(Had he, though?)

He clicked through them mechanically. Trust falls. Communication strategies. A deeply concerning section on "vulnerability as a leadership tool." An entire slide dedicated to the importance of "choosing joy."

By Slide 29, his eye was twitching.

By Slide 35, he was gripping the edge of his desk hard enough that his claws left marks in the wood.

Slide 37 featured a cartoon Santa and Krampus shaking hands beneath text that read: **TOGETHER, WE CREATE MAGIC!**

Krampus clicked COMPLETE with the energy of someone closing a coffin lid.

CONGRATULATIONS! the screen announced. **You've completed the first step toward meaningful collaborative growth! Your Goodwill Outreach assignment will arrive within 24-48 hours. Get ready for an exciting partnership opportunity!**

He closed the window.

The silence rushed back in. His own breathing. The ancient stones settled. The absence of anyone to commiserate with, to complain to, to share the absurdity of—

He cut the thought off.

Somewhere in the back of his mind, a question surfaced: *When was the last time you talked to Santa? Not through HR. Not through formal channels. Just... talked?*

He stood abruptly. Returned to his filing system. Pulled out the Stuttgart case. Put it back. His hands moved through the familiar motions—organize, categorize, file—but his mind kept drifting to the ornament in the locked drawer.

The coffee was still cold.

He did not bother making a fresh cup.

Chapter Two

THE PACKAGE

The box arrived shortly before 4 PM the following day.

Krampus heard it before he saw it: the telltale *whoompf* of interdimensional delivery, followed by the scrape of cardboard on stone as something materialized in the center of his lair.

He looked up from his desk.

A large crate sat there, stamped with the North Pole's official seal and wrapped in cheerful red ribbon that seemed to glow with barely contained magic. The label read:

FRAGILE - PARTNERSHIP MATERIALS - HANDLE WITH CARE.

Krampus approached it the way one might approach a suspicious package ticking ominously in a public square.

"Partnership materials," he muttered. "Probably team-building exercises. Or trust fall equipment."

He circled the crate once. It didn't move. Didn't make noise. Seemed harmless enough.

Maybe they'd sent him coal-related upgrades after all. New chains, perhaps. An updated birch rod with an ergonomic grip. Something useful that HR had disguised as "collaborative tools" to satisfy their bureaucratic nonsense.

He could work with that.

Krampus grabbed a crowbar from his workshop and pried open the lid.

The crate exploded.

Not literally—though given the geese incident of 1743, he wouldn't have been surprised—but with *movement*. A black blur launched itself out of the box, landed on his desk with the grace of a small apex predator, and immediately sat down. Stared at him. Blinked slowly.

It was a cat. A magnificent, absurdly fluffy cat with fur so black it seemed to absorb light, eyes that glowed an unsettling shade of amber, and the unmistakable energy of someone who knew *exactly* how much chaos they were about to cause and was deeply looking forward to it.

The cat's tail swished once.

Krampus stared back.

"No," he said.

The cat purred.

It was the loudest purr Krampus had ever heard. It rattled through the lair like distant thunder, echoing off the stone walls, vibrating in his chest.

"Absolutely not."

The cat stretched—long, luxurious, showing off razor-sharp claws that left tiny scratches on his desk's oak surface. Then it yawned, displaying an alarming number of teeth.

Krampus looked back at the crate.

A tag dangled from the inside lid, written in Santa's unmistakable handwriting:

> *For partnership development.*
> *P.S. His name is TBD. You'll figure*
> *it out.*
> *—S.C.*

"I don't want a cat," Krampus said aloud.

The cat responded by standing, padding across the desk with deliberate steps, and sitting directly on top of his naughty list filing index.

The one he'd just spent four hours updating. The one organized by twenty-three different criteria. The one that represented the culmination of decades of systematic optimization.

The cat looked him dead in the eye. Then, maintaining eye contact, it raised one paw and slowly—deliberately—pushed the entire index card box off the desk. It hit the floor with a catastrophic crash.

Five hundred meticulously organized index cards exploded across the stone floor in a cascade of color-coded chaos. Red cards mixed with yellow. Geographical regions scattered into behavioral categories. Cross-references were now separated from their primaries. Months of work. Gone.

The cat sat in the exact center of the desk, tail wrapped primly around its paws, and purred louder.

Krampus's eye twitched. "Get back in the box."

The cat regarded the box with profound indifference before resuming its grooming.

Krampus grabbed the crate, checking for return instructions. There had to be a return policy. Even Holiday HR wouldn't be cruel enough to make this permanent. Surely there was some clause, some loophole, some—

A piece of paper fluttered out of the crate's bottom.

PARTNERSHIP ASSIGNMENT CONFIRMATION
Entity Assigned: Spirit Companion (Feline)
Assignment Duration: Indefinite
Return Policy: NO RETURNS. NO EXCHANGES. NO REFUNDS.

Questions? Contact HR at your earliest convenience (Response time: 6-8 business weeks)

—*Management*

"No," Krampus said again, with more force.

The universe, as usual, did not care about his preferences.

He grabbed the crate, anyway, and shoved it toward the cat with clear intent.

The cat looked at the box. Looked at Krampus. Yawned again. Then it stepped delicately off the desk, sauntered across the floor —*through* the scattered index cards, naturally, leaving paw prints on several—and jumped onto the second chair. The one that hadn't been used in years.

It circled three times. Curled into a perfect ball of black fluff. And went to sleep. Just like that. As if it had always lived there. As if it belonged.

Krampus stood in the middle of his lair, surrounded by the wreckage of his filing system, staring at the sleeping cat that had invaded his space and destroyed his work in under three minutes.

The cat's purring continued, a low rumble that filled every corner of the silence.

Krampus closed his eyes. Counted to ten. Considered options: None of the options were good.

He opened his eyes. The cat was still there, still sleeping, still purring like a small, motorized engine of chaos. Fine.

Fine.

He'd survived the Black Plague. He'd survived five centuries of mortal ingratitude. He'd survived thirty-seven slides about synergy. He could survive one cat.

It would stay for a few days, realize this lair was terrible, and leave on its own. Cats were independent. Everyone knew that. This would resolve itself naturally.

Krampus knelt and began gathering the scattered index cards, trying not to notice how the cat's breathing had settled into an even rhythm, or how the lair suddenly didn't feel quite as silent as it had that morning.

He told himself the purring was annoying. He told himself this was temporary. He told himself he absolutely did not notice the way the cat had chosen the guest chair—*his* chair, from when partnership meant something—as if it somehow knew.

By the time he'd sorted the cards back into rough piles, the cat had been asleep for an hour.

Krampus made fresh coffee. Pretended everything was fine.

The cat purred on.

Chapter Three

SOMETHING'S WRONG

The bells started at midnight.

Krampus woke to the sound of jingling—faint at first, then growing louder. The familiar sound of his own bells, the ones he kept oiled and wrapped in cloth in the workshop. Except he could see them from his bed. Still wrapped. Still silent.

The jingling continued. He sat up. Listened.

The sound was coming from everywhere and nowhere at once. Echoing off the stone walls, bouncing through the corridors, emanating from the very air itself.

The cat sat in the doorway of his bedroom, silhouetted against the dim light from the main hall. Its eyes reflected an eerie glow. It was still purring.

"This is you," Krampus said.

The cat's tail swished once.

The bells got louder.

By morning, things had escalated.

Krampus stood at his window, watching snow fall *upward*.

Not drifting. Not swirling in wind patterns. Falling in reverse, flakes rising from the ground toward the sky in defiance of every natural law he'd witnessed in five centuries.

He blinked. Rubbed his eyes. The snow continued its impossible ascent.

"Stop that," he said to the cat, who was currently sitting on the windowsill, watching the backward snow with the interest of someone observing their own handiwork.

The cat did not stop it.

Krampus turned away, heading for his desk to document this new development. He managed three steps before he noticed his shadow.

It was moving wrong. Not following his movements—more like it was anticipating them. When he raised his hand, the shadow moved first. When he stepped left, the shadow had already shifted.

He stopped walking. The shadow stopped a half-second later.

"What," Krampus said slowly, "are you?"

The cat jumped down from the windowsill, landing without a sound. It padded across the room, hopped onto his desk, and sat directly on top of a book.

Krampus looked down.

Professional Distance: A Manual for Maintaining Appropriate Workplace Boundaries

The HR-mandated reading he'd been assigned last quarter. The one with an entire chapter on "why isolation is counterproductive to team dynamics."

The cat sat on it, unmoving, staring at him with those unsettling amber eyes.

"Move," Krampus said.

The cat purred.

"I need that book."

The cat settled more firmly onto it, somehow managing to increase its surface area.

"I don't have time for—"

A bell rang somewhere in the depths of the lair. Then another. Then a whole cascade of them, though Krampus could see his bells were still motionless in the workshop.

The cat's purr intensified.

Magic. The cat was a conduit for something. Some kind of supernatural interference that was bleeding into his lair, disrupting the natural order, causing chaos in what had been a perfectly organized, perfectly controlled environment.

He needed to contain it.

Krampus scooped the cat up—surprisingly warm, surprisingly solid—and carried it to the storage room. The one with reinforced doors. The one he used for particularly volatile magical items.

The cat went limp in his arms, completely relaxed, purring like a small earthquake.

"You're staying here," Krampus said, setting it down inside the room, "until I figure out what you are."

He closed the door. Turned the lock. Added a magical seal for good measure. Walked back to his desk.

The cat was sitting on it. On the *exact same book*.

Krampus stared. Looked back at the storage room. The door was still closed. Still locked. Still sealed.

The cat blinked slowly at him.

"How did you—"

It happened again.

He grabbed the cat, carried it back to the storage room, opened the door to confirm it was empty, placed the cat inside, closed and locked the door, added *two* magical seals this time, and walked back to his desk.

The cat was already there. Sitting on the manual. Purring.

"This is impossible," Krampus said.

The cat yawned.

He tried four more times. Four different rooms. Four different locks. One particularly ambitious attempt involving chains, a binding spell, and what was essentially a magical time-out corner.

Every time, the cat appeared behind him within seconds. Sometimes sitting on his desk. Sometimes on the guest chair. Once, memorably, sitting on his head. By the sixth attempt, Krampus gave up.

"Fine," he muttered, slumping into his desk chair. "You win. Stay wherever you want. Ruin everything. See if I care."

The cat, currently occupying the *Professional Distance* manual, purred in what sounded like approval.

Krampus pulled out a different book—one on cataloging systems—and tried to focus on his work. The bells were still ringing intermittently. The snow was still falling upward. His shadow was still moving independently.

But at least the cat was staying in one place. Small victories.

He was three pages into the cataloging chapter when he felt it. Warmth against his leg. Soft pressure. The vibration of purring.

The cat had jumped down from the desk and was rubbing against his leg, weaving between his ankles in a figure-eight pattern. Its fur was impossibly soft. The purr was impossibly loud.

And for one second—one single, traitorous second—Krampus felt something shift.

The lair didn't seem so empty. The silence didn't seem so absolute. The weight of five hundred years felt, somehow, less crushing.

He stood up so fast, his chair scraped backward across the stone floor.

The cat looked up at him, unperturbed.

Krampus stood there, breathing harder than the moment warranted, staring down at the creature that had invaded his space and was now invading something far more dangerous.

"No," he said.

The cat tilted its head.

"This doesn't mean anything."

The cat sat down.

"You're a conduit for magical interference. That's all. A temporary inconvenience. Nothing more."

The cat began grooming itself.

Krampus turned away, putting distance between them, trying to ignore the fact that his leg still felt warm where the cat had touched it.

He needed to organize something. File something. Restore order to—

The crash came from across the room.

He spun around.

The locked drawer, the one from the lower cabinet, the one he *never* opened—had somehow come open. Files and old record books were scattered across the floor.

And rolling slowly across the stone, wobbling on its round base, was the ornament.

The hand-carved one. The one with both their initials.

It rolled to a stop at the cat's feet. The cat looked down at it. Looked up at Krampus. Back down at the ornament. Then it reached out one paw and gently—*so gently*—touched it.

"Don't," Krampus said, crossing the room in three strides.

He snatched the ornament up before the cat could do whatever cats did with priceless emotional artifacts. Held it against his chest. His heart was pounding harder than it should have been.

The cat watched him. Those amber eyes seemed to see everything. The way his hands shook slightly. The way he couldn't quite bring himself to put the ornament back in the drawer yet. The way he stood there, five hundred years of carefully constructed emotional distance threatening to crack around one stupid piece of carved wood.

"You don't understand what this is," Krampus said quietly.

The cat slow-blinked. Somehow, that was worse than if it had looked away.

Krampus shoved the ornament into his pocket instead of the drawer. Gathered up the scattered files with hands that weren't quite steady.

His fingers brushed against something different. Stiffer. A sealed envelope, the paper expensive and formal, with his name written in a hand he would recognize anywhere.

His breath stopped.

For one sharp moment, he saw it again—the North Pole courier, three weeks after the inquiry, standing at his door with nervous eyes and an envelope that felt like a tombstone.

I miss working with you. Can we talk?

He'd never opened it. Couldn't open it. Because opening it meant knowing, and not knowing meant he could still pretend—

Krampus shoved the letter deeper into the pile. Covered it with obsolete record books. Forced himself not to look at the cat, who had settled back onto the guest chair and was watching him with the patience of something that had all the time in the world.

The bells rang again. The snow fell upward. His shadow moved independently.

And Krampus tried very hard not to think about how the lair had been silent for years, and now it was full of impossible sounds, impossible magic, and one impossible cat who had seen exactly what he'd been trying to hide.

The cat purred.

Krampus pretended not to hear it.

Chapter Four

THE QUESTION

Dawn arrived not with light, but with the materialization of a partridge.

One moment, Krampus was drinking his cold coffee—he'd given up reheating it—and the next, there was a bird in his kitchen.

Not a normal bird. This one *glowed*. Soft golden light emanated from its feathers, casting dancing shadows across the stone walls. It was the size of a small chicken, with plumage that shimmered as if dipped in liquid starlight.

It landed on the scattered index cards still covering his floor, the ones the cat had destroyed yesterday. It pecked at one marked "Stuttgart: Cryptocurrency Scheme" with apparent interest.

Then it looked up at Krampus.

Krampus looked back.

"No," he said.

The partridge ruffled its feathers and flew directly at his face.

He ducked. The bird soared over his head, made a graceful loop around the chandelier he did not have, and landed with surprising weight directly on top of his horns.

"Get off."

The partridge settled in, its talons gripping the grooves in his horns like they were custom-designed perches. Its weight was negligible, but its presence was loud. The glow intensified as the bird shifted, making itself comfortable.

Then it spoke.

"We need to talk about your life choices," the partridge said in a voice that sounded like a disappointed grandmother who had just discovered your report card.

Krampus froze. "You—"

"Yes, I talk. No, you don't get a say in this. I'm here for the next month, possibly longer depending on your progress, and we're going to have some *conversations*."

"Get. Off. My. Head."

"Your horns, technically. And no." The partridge leaned forward, peering down at him from its elevated perch. "Let's start with the obvious: when did you last feel joy?"

"I am calling HR."

"HR sent me. Well, technically the universe sent me via magical intervention triggered by your new roommate, but Holiday HR is very supportive of this process."

Krampus reached up to grab the bird.

It hopped to his other horn.

"Ah-ah. No touching. Clause 47-B of my

manifestation contract. Now, where were we? Oh yes. Joy. When was the last time you experienced it?"

"I experience professional satisfaction daily."

"That is not what I asked."

The cat, who had been watching this exchange from the guest chair with the focused intensity of a predator observing potential prey, suddenly stood. Its ears flattened. Its tail puffed to twice its normal size.

"Oh good," the partridge said. "The chaos agent has opinions. How delightful—"

The cat launched itself through the air with the grace of a furry missile.

The partridge shrieked and took flight.

What followed was three minutes of absolute mayhem.

The cat ricocheted off walls, furniture, and at one point Krampus himself, chasing the glowing bird through the lair with single-minded determination. The partridge dive-bombed and swooped, hurling what sounded like psychological assessments as it flew.

"Your attachment style is clearly avoidant!"

The cat knocked over a lamp.

"You've confused routine with purpose!"

A chair went skidding across the floor.

"When did isolation become your identity instead of a circumstance?"

The cat climbed the curtains Krampus did not remember having and launched itself at the bird with claws extended.

"ENOUGH!"

Krampus's voice echoed through the lair with enough force that both animals froze mid-chase.

The cat hung from the curtain rod, panting.

The partridge hovered in mid-air, its wings beating rapidly, glowing brighter in what might have been indignation.

"This is my lair," Krampus enunciated deliberately. "There are rules. No fighting. No property damage. No—"

A sound like cracking wood interrupted him. A deep groan from the very stones under his feet.

He turned slowly.

In the corner of his dining area—the small space where he kept his one table, the one he used for meals and paperwork and the occasional ritual that required a flat surface—something was growing.

A tree. A pear tree, specifically.

It sprouted from the stone floor as if the laws of nature were merely gentle suggestions. Roots cracked through rock with a sound like splintering bone. The trunk thickened, bark forming in a rush of fast-forward growth. Branches stretched outward with grasping fingers.

The table—his ONLY table—groaned under the sudden pressure.

"Stop," Krampus said.

The tree did not stop. It grew through the table. Wood splintered. The surface split down the middle as the trunk expanded, pushing the two halves apart like a ship breaking on rocks. Papers scattered. His coffee mug, the one he'd been using for seventy years, fell and shattered.

Branches spread across the ceiling. Pears began to form, swelling from green buds to golden fruit in seconds.

The table collapsed entirely.

Krampus stood amid the wreckage of his dining area, staring at the fully-grown pear tree that had just destroyed the only piece of furniture he had used daily for three centuries.

The partridge landed on a branch, preening.

"Lovely," it said. "Adds some life to the place. Very symbolic. Growth, renewal, the cyclical nature of—"

The cat jumped into the tree and resumed the chase.

"—POTENTIAL DEATH BY FELINE," the partridge finished, taking flight again.

Krampus closed his eyes. Counted to ten. Reached twenty. Kept going.

At thirty, he opened his eyes. The tree was still there. The table was still kindling. The cat and partridge were still engaged in aerial combat that was leaving feathers and claw marks across every surface.

He walked to the kitchen. Made more coffee. Returned to find the cat sitting victoriously on the highest branch while the partridge perched on a lower one, both of them now ignoring each other in a way that suggested a temporary truce.

"So," the partridge said, as if the last five minutes had not happened. "Back to my original question."

"I do not have to answer your questions."

"True. But I am not leaving until you do. That is rather the point of this whole exercise."

Krampus sat on the floor. His chair was somewhere under the pear tree's root system. His table was gone. His coffee was cold again.

The partridge hopped down to a lower branch, bringing itself to eye level.

"When did you last enjoy your work?" it asked. Not unkindly. Just... persistently.

Krampus opened his mouth. Closed it. He tried again. No words came.

He could not remember. Not the specific moment. Not even the general timeframe. There had been a point where the work mattered, where correction felt like care, where discipline was an act of hope rather than punishment.

But when had that been? A year ago? A decade? A century?

The silence stretched. The partridge waited.

The cat watched from its branch, its amber eyes reflecting the partridge's glow.

"I..." Krampus started. Stopped.

He set his coffee down on the floor because there was nowhere else to put it.

"That is what I thought," the partridge said quietly. Not triumphant. Just sad. "Well. We have a month to figure that out."

"A month?"

"I am the first day," the partridge said. "I will be here all month. The others will come and go, but me? I am permanent. Consider me your live-in therapist."

"I do not need therapy."

The partridge looked pointedly at the destroyed table, the scattered files that still had not been properly reorganized since the cat's arrival, the cold coffee, the lair that had nothing warm or living in it except a tree that had forced its way through solid stone.

"Right," it said. "You're doing great. Very healthy. No notes."

Krampus wanted to argue. He could not find the energy.

The cat descended from the tree, landing on his shoulder with a weight that should have hurt but somehow did not. It rubbed its head against his jaw, purring.

The partridge settled onto a branch that hung directly over where his table used to be.

A pear fell, landing with a soft thud on the scattered wood.

"I hate this," Krampus muttered.

"I know," the partridge said. "That is why it's working."

The cat purred louder.

Krampus sat on the floor of his lair, surrounded by chaos, and tried not to think about the fact that he genuinely could not remember the last time his work had felt like anything other than obligation.

The partridge began preening again, making itself comfortable.

"Welcome to Day One," it said cheerfully. "Only eleven more to go."

Outside, the snow continued falling upward.

Chapter Five

THE DIAGNOSIS

Krampus woke to the sound of cooing.

Soft, gentle, relentlessly cheerful cooing.

He opened his eyes.

The pear tree had grown overnight. Branches now stretched into his bedroom, one thick limb reaching across the doorway like an invasion. Two doves sat on that branch directly above his bed, perfectly perched among the impossible fruit. They were immaculate---soft gray plumage with subtle iridescent shimmers, eyes that radiated an unsettling combination of compassion and determination.

"Good morning, Krampus," the first one said in a voice like warm honey. "We're here to help."

"Out," Krampus said.

"We understand you're resistant to the process," the second dove said, somehow making it sound like a therapeutic observation rather than a statement of fact. "That's perfectly normal. Many individuals struggle with accepting support."

"OUT."

"We sense deep isolation," the first dove continued, tilting its head in that way therapists do when they're about to say something they think is profound. "A disconnection from authentic relationship that has calcified into—"

Krampus threw his pillow at them.

Both doves took flight, easily dodging the projectile, and landed on his dresser.

"Physical expressions of frustration often mask emotional vulnerability," the second dove observed.

"I will roast you," Krampus said.

"Threats of harm frequently indicate—"

"With rosemary and garlic."

"—a fear of intimacy."

Krampus got out of bed, pulled on his robe, and walked to the kitchen. The doves followed, flying in perfect synchronization, landing on the counter as he reached for the coffee.

"Tell us, Krampus," the first dove said, "When did you last have a meaningful conversation?"

"I'm not doing this."

"With someone other than yourself," the second dove clarified.

He poured coffee. The doves hopped closer, invading his personal space with the confidence of creatures who believed they were helping.

"Do you have a support network?" the first dove asked.

"No."

"Friends? Confidants? Anyone you trust with your authentic self?"

"No."

"Family you're in contact with?"

"No."

"Professional colleagues you socialize with outside of work obligations?"

"Absolutely not."

Both doves exchanged a look that managed to convey deep concern and professional consultation simultaneously.

"That's what we thought," the second dove said gently. "Krampus, isolation of this magnitude isn't sustainable. The mortal mind requires—"

"I'm not mortal."

"The *immortal* mind requires social connection even more so. Eternity without companionship leads to calcification of the soul, rigidity of perspective, and an inability to experience—"

Krampus walked to his desk. The doves followed, landing on the scattered files he still hadn't fully reorganized.

He sat down. They hopped onto his armrests.

"Let's talk about your relationship patterns," the first dove said.

"No."

"Have you considered that your professional role has become enmeshed with your identity in ways that prevent authentic connection?"

"No."

"When someone expresses care toward you, how do you typically respond?"

"I don't."

"Exactly," the second dove said, as if he'd just proven their point. "You deflect. You are isolated. You've constructed walls so high that even *you've* forgotten what they're protecting."

Krampus tried to read a report. The doves moved to sit directly on the paper.

"Your attachment style," the first dove continued, "appears to be dismissive-avoidant with elements of—"

"I'm working."

"Are you, though? Or are you *performing* work to avoid confronting the emptiness of—"

He stood up. Walked to the filing cabinets. The doves flew alongside him like the world's most earnest escort.

"Tell us about your last meaningful relationship," the second dove said.

Krampus pulled open a drawer. Stared at the files without seeing them.

"I don't have relationships."

"Past relationships, then."

"I don't discuss the past."

"Ah," both doves said in unison, with the satisfied tone of therapists who'd just found the wound.

"That deflection itself is meaningful," the first dove said. "The past clearly holds significant—"

"I'm going to the workshop."

He crossed the lair. The doves followed. Landed on his workbench as he tried to oil a chain.

"Do you ever feel lonely?" the second dove asked.

"No."

"Not even late at night when the silence becomes—"

"No."

"What about when you see others experiencing connection and wonder what it would be like to—"

"*No.*"

"Denial," the first dove said to the second, "is often the—"

Krampus slammed the oil can down hard enough to make both doves jump.

"I am not in denial. I am not lonely. I do not need companionship. I *prefer* solitude. I have *chosen* this life. Just because *you* can't comprehend someone genuinely wanting to be alone doesn't mean there's something *wrong* with me."

The doves waited until he'd finished. Then they looked at each other. Then back at him.

"The vehemence of that response," the second dove said carefully, "suggests—"

"GET OUT!"

"—deep-seated pain that manifests as defensive—"

Krampus grabbed a broom.

The doves took flight, circling near the ceiling, still talking.

"It's okay to want companionship, Krampus," the first dove called down. "It's a natural need. Nothing to be ashamed of."

"I don't *want* it."

"Humans—"

"Not human."

"—*beings* require connection. It's not weakness. It's biology. Psychology. Basic—"

Something warm and heavy landed in his lap. Krampus looked down.

The cat had somehow materialized there, curled into an impossibly compact ball of black fluff. The purr started immediately, vibrating through his legs, up his spine, filling the space around them.

The cat looked up at him with half-closed eyes. Blinked slowly. Settled its head on its paws. The purr intensified.

The doves landed on the pear tree, watching.

"See?" the first dove said softly. "You do have companionship."

"...This doesn't count."

"He's sitting on your lap."

"He just shows up places. I didn't ask for this."

"You also haven't removed him."

Krampus looked down at the cat. The cat's eyes were fully closed now, its breathing deep and even, completely relaxed in a way that suggested absolute trust.

His hand hovered over the cat's back. He didn't quite touch.

"I could move him," Krampus said.

"But you won't," the second dove observed.

"He'd just come back."

"Would he? Or do you *want* him to come back?"

"I—" Krampus stopped. "This is manipulation."

"This is observation."

The cat shifted, pressing more firmly into his lap. One paw extended, pushing against his stomach in a gentle kneading motion.

The purr got louder.

"It's okay," the first dove said, "to want companionship."

"I don't," Krampus said, but his voice had lost its conviction.

The cat purred.

His hand lowered, hovering just above the soft black fur.

"Denial," the second dove said gently, "is the first stage."

Krampus's hand clenched into a fist. He looked up at the doves with an expression that had made mortals flee screaming.

"I am not in denial. This animal appeared in my home uninvited. The fact that it refuses to leave and has apparently decided I am furniture does *not* constitute a relationship. It's a parasite. A particularly fluffy, loud parasite that—"

The cat rolled over, exposing its belly, still purring.

"—has no respect for personal space or professional boundaries or—"

One of the doves tilted its head.

"—the clearly stated preference for solitude that I have maintained for *three hundred years* and—"

His hand was on the cat's stomach now. He didn't remember moving it.

The fur was impossibly soft. The purr was impossibly loud. The warmth was seeping into his palm, up his arm, into his chest where something tight had lived for longer than he cared to admit.

"This doesn't mean anything," Krampus said quietly.

The doves said nothing.

The cat purred.

The partridge, watching from a higher branch, made a small approving sound.

Krampus sat there, hand on the cat's belly, surrounded by magical creatures who had invaded his home and his space and his carefully maintained isolation, and tried to remember when he'd decided that being alone was the same thing as being safe.

The doves settled onto the pear tree branches.

"We'll be here if you want to talk," the first one said.

"I won't."

"We'll be here anyway," the second one said.

The cat stretched, all four paws extending, claws flexing against Krampus's robe. Then it curled back into a ball and went to sleep.

Krampus's hand stayed where it was. His jaw clenched so hard it hurt. His other hand gripped the arm of his chair tight enough that his claws left grooves in the wood.

Every muscle in his body was tense, screaming at him to stand up, to move, to *stop this* before it became something he couldn't take back. But he didn't move.

The cat purred.

The doves watched with the patience of creatures who knew they'd already won.

And Krampus sat there, hand on the cat's warm belly, and pretended this was fine. Pretended he was still in control. Pretended he didn't notice how the lair felt different with a purring weight in his lap.

Outside, the snow fell upward. The bells rang. His shadow moved independently.

And somewhere deep in the filing cabinets, in a drawer he never opened, an ornament waited.

Chapter Six

THE UNION

The hens arrived in a cloud of scarlet feathers and indignation.

One moment, Krampus was attempting to drink his coffee in peace—the cat still in his lap, the doves perched on the pear tree branches offering unsolicited observations about his "emotional growth trajectory" and the next, three magnificent chickens materialized on his filing cabinets.

They were spectacular. Russet and gold plumage that caught the light, eyes sharp with intelligence, posture that suggested they'd studied classical theater and took themselves very seriously.

The largest one surveyed the lair with the critical eye of a director reviewing a disappointing set.

"*Mon Dieu*," she said, her accent thick and dramatic. "This is the workplace?"

"I..." Krampus started.

"Do not answer yet. I am still processing the tragedy before me." She spread her wings in a gesture that looked rehearsed. "Colette! Brigitte! Bear witness to these conditions!"

The other two hens clucked in synchronized dismay.

"No windows!" the second hen—Colette—declared.

"No warmth!" added Brigitte.

"No *aesthetic consideration whatsoever!*" the first hen finished, as if this were the gravest sin of all.

Krampus set down his coffee. "Who—"

"I am Vivienne," the first hen announced, standing taller. "And we are here to work, *oui*? To fulfill our role in this... this *spectacle* of holiday magic. But we are not *peasants*. We have standards. Dignity. Rights!"

"You've been here thirty seconds."

"Thirty seconds too long in these conditions!" Vivienne hopped to a different cabinet, examining it like a health inspector finding violations. "Look at this filing system. Functional, *oui*, but where is the *joie de vivre*? Where is the color? The life?"

"It's color-coded," Krampus said.

All three hens gasped as if he'd admitted to a crime.

"Color-coded for *efficiency*," Vivienne said, shaking her head. "Not for beauty. Not for joy. This is the problem with modern workplace culture. Always the optimization, never the *soul*."

She turned to the other hens. "Sisters! We must convene."

The three chickens huddled together on top of the filing cabinet, whispering in rapid French. Occasionally one would gesture dramatically toward different parts of the lair. Another would shake her head with theatrical sadness.

The cat, still in Krampus's lap, watched with the fascinated attention of a predator observing strange new prey.

After exactly four minutes, the hens broke their huddle.

Vivienne cleared her throat. "We have reached a decision," she announced. "We will work, *oui*, but not under these conditions. We have demands."

"Demands."

"*Oui*. Number one: a heated coop. Not excessive heat, we are not asking for luxury. Simply basic workplace comfort."

"You don't work here—"

"Number two!" Colette interjected. "Hazard pay. We have observed the partridge. We have seen the chaos agent." She gestured toward the cat. "This is clearly a hostile work environment."

"Number three," Brigitte added, "dignity. We will not be treated as mere decorative elements. We are skilled professionals with—"

"You're chickens."

Three sets of sharp eyes turned on him.

"We," Vivienne said with icy precision, "are French hens. There is a difference. We bring culture. Sophistication. An appreciation for beauty that this..." she gestured vaguely at the entire lair, "...this *dungeon* clearly lacks."

"It's not a dungeon. It's a lair."

"The distinction," Colette said, "is minimal."

Krampus looked at the doves, who seemed to be enjoying this immensely.

"Are they always like this?" he asked.

"You're asking *us* about difficult houseguests?" the first dove said.

Vivienne hopped down from the filing cabinet, landing on Krampus's desk with surprising grace. She walked directly up to a stack of paperwork and examined it.

"Tell me, Krampus," she said, her voice shifting from indignant to genuinely curious. "Do you enjoy this work?"

"We've covered this already," the partridge called from its branch. "Answer is no."

"I did not ask the bird," Vivienne said sharply. "I asked the demon."

Krampus opened his mouth. Closed it.

"Because," Vivienne continued, strutting across his desk, "I see here a workplace devoid of pleasure. Of satisfaction. Of *anything* that makes the labor worthwhile. This is not sustainable, *non?*"

"I sustain fine."

"You *survive*," Colette corrected, having hopped down to join Vivienne. "Survival is not the same as living."

"We refuse," Brigitte declared, completing the trio on his desk, "to work in an environment devoid of joy. It is against our principles."

"Your principles."

"*Oui*. We are French. We have many principles. Chief among them: beauty matters. Joy matters. Even Hell should have *some* beauty, *non*?"

Krampus stared at the three chickens who had invaded his workspace and were now lecturing him about aesthetics.

"It's efficient," he said.

"Efficiency," Vivienne said sadly, "is not enough. When did you last have something here just because it made you happy?"

The question hung in the air.

The doves leaned forward from their branches.

The partridge stopped preening.

Even the cat, still purring in his lap, seemed to pause.

Krampus looked around his lair. The bare stone walls. The functional furniture, most of it now destroyed by a pear tree. The filing cabinets organized by region and severity. The calendar marking days. The single coffee mug.

The drawer he kept locked.

"I don't..." he started. Stopped. He tried again. "The work is what matters. Personal happiness is—"

"Is what?" Colette asked gently. "Secondary? Frivolous? Too much to ask for after five hundred years of service?"

"I—"

His hand was still resting on the cat. The purr vibrated through his palm. When had he started petting it? The motion was automatic now, his thumb stroking along the cat's spine in a rhythm he hadn't consciously chosen.

"The work matters," he said finally. "But I..."

The hens waited.

"I don't know when I stopped caring about anything else."

The admission came out quieter than he'd intended. Fell into the silence like a stone into deep water.

Vivienne's head tilted.

"*Voilà*," she said softly. "Progress."

"This is not progress. This is three chickens harassing me about interior decoration—"

"About *beauty*," Vivienne corrected. "About joy. About the small things that make existence bearable."

"I don't need—"

The cat suddenly stood up, stretched, and jumped from his lap to the desk. It walked directly to Vivienne, regarded her with those unsettling amber eyes, then sat down.

And knocked a pen off the desk. Then another. Then an entire stack of unfiled reports.

"Ah!" Brigitte said delightedly. "The chaos agent agrees with us!"

The cat jumped to the filing cabinet, pawed at a drawer until it opened, and pulled out a random file with its teeth.

"Stop that," Krampus said, standing.

The cat dropped the file, batted it across the floor, then turned and purred at the hens as if to say *See? Chaos.*

But then it did something strange. It jumped back to Krampus, landed on his shoulder, and began working its way around his neck. The weight settled. The purr intensified. Within seconds, the cat had arranged itself like a living scarf, draped across his shoulders, black fur stark against his dark robe.

Krampus froze. The purr rumbled directly against his collarbone. The cat's head rested against the side of his neck.

"I..." he said.

The hens had gone very quiet.

He looked over to find all three of them watching with identical expressions. Not smug. Not triumphant. Just... knowing.

Vivienne glanced at Colette.

Colette glanced at Brigitte.

Brigitte glanced back at Vivienne.

The same thought passed between them, visible in the slight tilt of their heads, the soft cluck of understanding.

"*Bien sûr*," Vivienne murmured. "He does not know yet."

"Know what?" Krampus demanded.

The cat purred louder, shifting to get more comfortable, one paw pressing lightly against his chest as if claiming territory.

"Nothing," Colette said innocently. "We know nothing."

"Absolutely nothing," Brigitte agreed.

"Merely that," Vivienne said, hopping off the desk and strutting toward the pear tree, "you are perhaps not as alone as you insist on being. And perhaps—*perhaps*—this is not entirely unwelcome."

"I didn't—"

"The chaos agent chose your shoulders," Vivienne said. "Not the chair. Not the desk. Not the lovely pear tree. You."

"He just shows up places. It doesn't mean—"

All three hens exchanged another look.

"*Oui, oui,*" Vivienne said. "It means nothing. Keep telling yourself this."

The cat purred.

Krampus's hand came up automatically to steady the cat's weight, fingers sinking into the soft fur. He caught himself. Froze.

"This doesn't—"

"Count," the first dove finished from its branch. "Yes, we've heard."

"Denial!" the second dove added cheerfully.

"Is the first stage," the partridge concluded.

Krampus stood in the center of his lair, wearing a cat like a scarf, surrounded by judgmental birds who had somehow turned his home into a referendum on his entire existence.

The hens settled on various perches, Vivienne on the pear tree, Colette on the filing cabinet, Brigitte on the guest chair.

"We will stay," Vivienne announced, "until this workplace meets basic standards of beauty and joy."

"I'm not redecorating."

"We shall see."

"I'm not—"

The cat shifted, rubbing its head against his jaw. The purr intensified. His hand was still in the fur.

The hens noticed. They noticed *everything*.

"*Petit à petit*," Vivienne said to her sisters. "Little by little."

"What does that mean?"

"It means," Colette said, "we are patient. We are French. We understand that some battles are won slowly."

"There is no battle—"

"Of course not," Brigitte said. "No battle. You are simply a demon who now wears a purring scarf and claims to want nothing."

"*Très tragique*," Vivienne sighed. "Very tragic."

The cat purred.

Krampus gave up. He walked to his desk—what remained of it—and tried to work with a cat draped across his shoulders and three French chickens offering commentary on everything from his filing methodology to his "clearly unresolved emotional baggage."

Outside, the snow fell upward. The bells rang. His shadow moved independently.

And Krampus tried very hard not to notice

how the weight around his neck felt less like an intrusion and more like—

He cut the thought off.

The cat purred.

The hens watched.

And somewhere in the chaos of magical birds and impossible weather, something in the lair's silence had started to change.

Chapter Seven

THE RECONNECTION

A burst of aggressive chirping at 6 AM announced the arrival of four identical black birds.

Sleek, black, and identical except for subtle variations in their tail feathers. They, they materialized on various surfaces around the lair —one on the filing cabinet, one on the pear tree, one on the guest chair, and one directly on Krampus's head.

Before he could react, the first bird opened its beak.

A phone rang. Not from the bird's mouth— though that would have made a certain kind of sense given the week he was having. The sound came from *everywhere*. A shrill, old-fashioned telephone ring that echoed off the stone walls.

A rotary phone materialized on his desk.

Krampus stared at it. It kept ringing.

"Answer it," the partridge called from its branch.

"I don't—"

Another bird opened its beak and a second

phone rang, this one a modern cell phone, with a digital chirp. It appeared on the filing cabinet.

"What is—"

A third bird, a third phone—this one with the frantic buzzing of a switchboard—materialized on the kitchen counter.

The fourth bird opened its beak and somehow, impossibly, a phone rang from inside the walls themselves.

"STOP," Krampus said.

All four phones continued their jarring chorus.

The cat, who had been sleeping on the guest chair, sat up and stared at the nearest phone with the focused intensity of something about to commit violence.

"Do not—" Krampus started.

The cat batted the phone off the filing cabinet. It hit the floor. It kept ringing.

"I don't have time for—"

One of the calling birds hopped to the rotary phone on his desk and, using only its beak and talons, picked up the receiver.

"HELLO?" a voice boomed from the speaker. "IS THIS THE MYTHIC TELECOMMUNICATIONS BUREAU? I NEED TO FILE A COMPLAINT ABOUT—"

The bird hung up. It immediately dialed again.

"What are you doing?" Krampus demanded.

The bird's eyes gleamed with mischief as the call connected.

"Yello?" said a voice that sounded ancient and vaguely Scandinavian.

"Who is—" Krampus started.

"IS THIS LOKI?" the calling bird shrieked into the phone.

"Oh, for the love of—hang up. HANG UP."

"WE'RE CALLING ABOUT YOUR EXTENDED WARRANTY—"

There was a sound like distant thunder, followed by creative cursing in Old Norse.

The line went dead. The bird immediately started dialing again.

Meanwhile, the second calling bird picked up the cell phone and began pecking at it with alarming precision.

"Stop that. Whatever you're doing, stop—"

"Hello?" said a bewildered voice from the cell phone speaker. "USPS customer service, this is Derek. How can I help you today?"

"HELLO DEREK," the bird screeched. "WE NEED TO DISCUSS PACKAGE DELIVERY TO SUPERNATURAL LOCATIONS—"

"I... what?"

"SPECIFICALLY HELL. DO YOU DELIVER TO HELL?"

"Sir, I think you have the wrong—"

"I'M A BIRD."

"...I'm going to transfer you to my supervisor."

Elevator music began playing from the cell phone.

The third calling bird had somehow

conference-called two different entities who were now arguing with each other through the switchboard phone.

"—telling you, the solstice celebration is on the 21st—"

"—IT'S THE 22ND, YOU ABSOLUTE FOOL—"

"—I checked the OFFICIAL CELESTIAL CALENDAR—"

Krampus grabbed for the rotary phone. The calling bird danced away, taking the receiver with it.

"Give me that."

The bird kept dialing. This time, when the call connected, there was a pause.

Then: "North Pole, how may I direct your call?"

Krampus froze.

"HELLO," the calling bird shrieked. "WE'D LIKE TO SPEAK TO SANTA CLAUS REGARDING—"

Krampus snatched the phone away. "This isn't—I didn't authorize—"

"One moment please," the receptionist said cheerfully.

"NO. No moment. Don't transfer—"

A click.

"Ho ho... Krampus? Is that you?"

Santa's voice. Warm. Familiar. Cautiously friendly in a way that suggested he was bracing for an argument.

Krampus's hand tightened on the receiver. He

turned away from the watching birds—all of them, the partridge, the doves, the hens, even the chaos-causing calling birds had paused to observe.

"This wasn't my idea," Krampus said.

"I figured. Magical interference again?"

"There are birds. Four of them. Making unauthorized calls to—"

"How's the cat?"

The question derailed his entire complaint.

"What?"

"The cat," Santa repeated. "How's he doing?"

Krampus looked over at the cat, who was currently sitting on top of the cell phone, pinning it to the desk while Derek from USPS continued holding in the background.

"Terrible," Krampus said. "It's destroying everything. My filing system. My furniture. Any semblance of order or peace or—"

"Good."

"GOOD?!"

"Yep." Santa sounded entirely too pleased. "That's exactly what I was hoping for."

"You *sent* me an agent of chaos as a partnership exercise?!"

"I sent you a friend."

"I don't need—"

"You named him yet?"

Krampus's mouth snapped shut. His eyes went to the cat again. The cat looked back, amber eyes half-closed, tail swishing lazily.

"...No," Krampus said.

"You will."

"I absolutely will not."

"Mmm." Santa hummed in that way he did when he knew something you didn't. "We'll see. Listen, I've got a situation with the elves—something about union negotiations and hazard pay—"

"The French hens," Krampus muttered.

"What?"

"Nothing."

"Right. Well. Keep me posted on the cat situation. And Krampus?"

"What."

A pause. Long enough that Krampus nearly asked if the connection had dropped.

"It's good to hear your voice," Santa said quietly. "It's been a while since we actually talked."

Something caught in Krampus's throat.

It had been. But he couldn't say that. Not after the formal inquiries, the memos, the way Santa had looked at him after the Plague—like he was a risk that needed to be managed rather than a partner who had made a mistake.

His hand moved on the receiver. He almost said something. Almost—

Click. The line went dead.

Krampus stood there, phone pressed to his ear, listening to the dial tone.

His other hand had come up at some point, reaching for something that wasn't there. An old gesture from when conversations with Santa had been natural instead of channeled through HR intermediaries and formal quarterly reviews.

When had that stopped?

The dial tone continued its lonely monotone.

"Well," the first dove said gently from its branch, "that seemed significant."

Krampus hung up the phone with more force than necessary.

He turned to find every bird in the lair watching him.

"It wasn't," he said.

"The call lasted four minutes," the partridge observed. "You didn't yell once after the first minute. Your posture relaxed. You almost smiled at the end."

"I did not—"

"Almost," the partridge repeated. "Before he hung up."

Krampus wanted to argue. He could not find the energy.

The cat jumped from the desk to his shoulder, that now-familiar weight settling across his neck. It started purring directly into his ear.

He reached up automatically to steady it, his hand sinking into the fur.

"You will name him," one of the French hens said from the pear tree. "*Éventuellement.* Eventually."

"I won't."

But his mind was already cycling through possibilities. Old words. Ancient names. Things that meant chaos or mischief or—

He cut the thought off. Focused on the continuing phone chaos instead.

Derek from USPS was still on hold, elevator music now accompanied by occasional confused questions about whether supernatural entities qualified for priority shipping.

The switchboard phone had somehow connected to something that sounded like it was conducting a meeting in a language that predated human civilization.

And the fourth calling bird, the one whose phone rang from within the walls, had apparently reached someone named Brenda.

"—so I said to him, I said, 'If you're going to reorganize the entire pantry, at least tell me where you put the paprika,'" Brenda was saying. "And does he? No. Never does. Forty-three years of marriage and I still can't find anything in my own kitchen."

The calling bird made sympathetic chirping sounds.

"You're sweet to listen, dear. Most people don't want to hear about my pantry situation. Are you sure you're a bird? You sound very understanding for a bird."

More chirping.

"Well, you're lovely company. Now, what was it you called about?"

The bird tilted its head, apparently having forgotten.

"That's alright, sweetie. Sometimes I call people and forget why too. Would you like to hear about my grandson? He just started college…"

Krampus looked at the rotary phone on his desk. His hand hovered over it.

He could call Santa back. Ask about those union negotiations. Offer to send the French hens to the North Pole since they were clearly the cause. Have an actual conversation instead of—

The cat's purr intensified, as if sensing the direction of his thoughts.

"I'm not calling him back," Krampus said aloud.

"No one suggested you should," the second dove said.

"I'm not."

"Of course not."

"It was a brief, meaningless exchange mandated by magical interference. Nothing more."

"Absolutely nothing more," the partridge agreed in a tone that suggested it absolutely was something more.

Krampus sat down at his desk. The cat adjusted its position across his shoulders, draping more comfortably. Heavy. Warm. Still purring.

His hand reached for files. Stopped. Reached for his coffee instead. Also cold. It was always cold now.

He reached for the phone. Stopped.

He looked at the cat, currently using his shoulder as a bed.

Opened his mouth. "Your name isn't..." he started.

The cat's eyes opened slightly.

"I'm not naming you."

The cat blinked slowly.

"But if I were to name you—which I am not—it wouldn't be something ridiculous. Nothing cute. Nothing that suggests... attachment or..."

The cat's purr got louder.

"Something practical," Krampus continued, despite himself. "Something that describes what you are. Chaos. Mayhem. Catastrophe. Calamity..."

None of them fit.

The cat shifted, pressing its head against his jaw.

"Yule," Krampus said quietly. Then stopped. "No. I didn't— That's not—"

But the word had already escaped. It had already settled into the air between them like a truth he couldn't take back.

The cat purred louder.

"I'm not using that," Krampus said quickly. "I was just... thinking aloud. Testing sounds. It doesn't mean—"

"*Yule*," Vivienne repeated from her branch, savoring the word. "*C'est parfait*. Very fitting."

"I didn't name him."

"Of course not," Colette said.

"You just said a word," Brigitte added. "A word that happens to fit perfectly. A word that just happens to be what one calls the winter solstice celebration. Very coincidental."

"Denial," both doves said in unison.

"Is the first stage," the partridge finished.

Krampus gripped the edge of his desk.

The cat—*Yule*, his mind supplied traitorously—purred and settled more firmly across his shoulders.

Brenda was still talking to the calling bird, now explaining her recipe for pot roast.

Derek from USPS had apparently given up and was just letting the elevator music play.

The switchboard phone had somehow connected to what sounded like a very confused deity trying to figure out who had called them at 6 AM about "seasonal synergy initiatives."

And Krampus sat in the center of the chaos, wearing a cat he had not named, surrounded by birds he had not invited, trying not to think about the fact that Santa's voice had sounded genuinely happy to talk to him.

Outside, the snow fell upward. The bells rang. His shadow moved independently.

And somewhere in his mind, a name had taken root despite every effort to prevent it.

Yule.

The cat purred.

Krampus pretended this was fine.

Chapter Eight

THE MEMORY

He woke to find the space beneath Yule occupied by five golden rings, glinting in the dawn light where only blanket had been before.

Krampus noticed them when he woke to find the cat—*not named, he kept telling himself, just a designation for organizational purposes*—had migrated from the guest chair to his bed sometime during the night.

Yule was curled into a tight ball at the foot of the bed, purring in sleep. Underneath him, glinting in the early light, were five golden rings.

Not small. Each one was the size of a bracelet, thick and ornate, covered in inscriptions that seemed to shift when looked at directly. They glowed with a soft, pulsing light that made the air around them feel warm.

Wrong. Everything about them felt wrong.

Krampus sat up carefully, trying not to disturb Yule. Leaned closer to examine the rings without touching them.

The inscriptions were moving. Forming words in languages he recognized: Joy. Delight.

Cheer. Happiness. Over and over, cycling through variations, glowing brighter with each repetition.

"Those are cursed," the partridge announced from the doorway.

Krampus jumped. "How long have you been watching?"

"Long enough to tell you not to touch those. Seriously. Don't touch them."

"I wasn't planning to—"

Yule woke up, stretched, and stood. The rings scattered across the bed as he moved, rolling in different directions.

One rolled directly toward Krampus's hand.

"Don't—" the partridge started.

Krampus jerked his hand back. The ring kept rolling. Hit the edge of the bed. Bounced. Landed on his bare foot.

"—touch it," the partridge finished. "Too late."

The effect was immediate. Warmth flooded through him, starting at his foot and rushing upward like someone had injected sunlight directly into his veins. His chest expanded. His face muscles moved in ways they hadn't moved in—how long? Decades? Centuries?

He was smiling. Not a polite grimace. Not a sarcastic smirk. An actual, genuine smile that reached his eyes and made his whole face feel strange and light.

"Oh no," the partridge said.

"Good morning!" Krampus said brightly, standing up and stretching. "What a beautiful day! Well, relatively speaking. The snow's still going the wrong direction, but honestly, it's kind of charming when you think about it. Like the universe decided to shake things up a bit!"

Yule's ears flattened.

"Is the ceiling leaking again?" Krampus continued, noticing a wet spot on the stone. "You know what, that's fine! We'll just put a bucket there. Problem solved! Everything's fixable with a little creativity and a positive attitude!"

The partridge flew to the pear tree where the other birds were gathering, all of them staring.

"What happened to him?" Colette whispered.

"Cursed rings," the partridge said. "Aggressive cheerfulness. I tried to warn him."

"How long does it last?" Vivienne asked.

"Hours. Maybe days. Depends on the curse strength."

Krampus was now humming while making coffee. Actually *humming*. A cheerful little tune that echoed through the lair.

"This is disturbing," Brigitte muttered.

"This is *fascinating*," the first dove said, leaning forward. "We're seeing who he was before the cynicism calcified."

Krampus poured his coffee, took a sip, and smiled even though it was cold.

"You know what?" he said to no one in particular. "Cold coffee is underrated. It's refreshing! Invigorating! Why heat it when you can just appreciate it as is?"

He walked to his desk, stepping over the

scattered index cards he still hadn't fully reorganized, and instead of his usual growl of frustration, he just laughed.

"Look at this mess! This is what life looks like when you're actually living it instead of obsessing over perfect order. This is *great!*"

Yule jumped onto the desk, watching him with those amber eyes.

Krampus reached out and scratched behind the cat's ears without hesitation, without the usual half-second of resistance.

"And you!" he said warmly. "You magnificent little chaos agent. You know what? I'm glad you're here. You're exactly what this place needed. What *I* needed. A little disorder. A little warmth. A little—"

He stopped. Looked at his hand, buried in Yule's fur. Kept petting.

"—companionship," he finished quietly, but still with that cursed cheer threading through his voice. "Even if I've been too stubborn to admit it."

"*Sacré bleu,*" Vivienne breathed. "The curse is revealing truth."

Krampus turned to his files, pulling out the Stuttgart case—the cryptocurrency scheme child.

"You know what this kid needs?" he said, reading the report. "Guidance. Not punishment. Not terror. Someone to sit down and explain *why* what they're doing is wrong and help them find a better path. Someone to actually care about their development instead of just—"

He stopped again. Set the file down. His smile faltered for half a second, then returned full force.

"I used to do that," he said, more to himself than the watching birds. "I used to care about the *why*. About helping them understand. When did I stop?"

Before anyone could answer, there was a knock at the door.

Krampus never had visitors.

He opened it to find a lost soul—literally, a translucent figure wrapped in chains of their own making, wandering the space between worlds, looking for direction.

"Oh!" Krampus said brightly. "Hello there! You look lost. Can I help you find your way?"

The soul stared at him. "You're... Krampus?"

"I am! And you look like you've been wandering for a while. Here, let me—" He stepped outside, gesturing for the soul to follow. "See that path there? The one with the light at the end? That's your way forward. You've been stuck because you're still carrying guilt about—" He paused, looking at the chains. "—about choices you made. But here's the thing: you don't have to carry those anymore. You can set them down. You can choose differently now."

"I can?" The soul's voice was small.

"Of course you can. That's the whole point. Growth. Change. Redemption. You're not stuck being who you were. You can choose who you want to become."

The soul's chains began to shimmer.

"Really?" they whispered.

"Really," Krampus said, and his smile was genuine, warm, the kind of expression that suggested he actually cared about this being's journey. "You've got this. I believe in you."

The soul started crying. Not sad tears—relieved ones.

"Thank you," they sobbed. "Thank you. I've been lost for so long and everyone just... walked past. No one stopped. No one cared. But you—"

"Hey," Krampus said gently, reaching out like he might touch their shoulder but stopping just short. "You matter. Your journey matters. Don't forget that."

The soul nodded, still crying, and moved toward the path. The chains fell away as they walked, dissolving into light.

Krampus watched them go, his smile soft. Then he turned and came back inside.

All the birds were silent.

"What?" he said cheerfully. "That felt good! Why don't I do that more often? That used to be the whole point of this job! Not just punishment, but guidance. Care. Actually, helping people find their way instead of just—"

The memory hit without warning.

He was back in the old workshop—the real one, before the rebrand, before the corporate restructuring. The air was thick with pine shavings and hot metal.

Santa was beside him, bent over a workbench, his laugh echoing off timbered ceilings as they guided a newly-formed winter spirit toward its purpose. The spirit had been lost, confused, terrified of its own power. Krampus had knelt beside it—when had he stopped kneeling?—and explained gently what it was, what it could become. Santa's hand had landed warm on his shoulder. "That's it," Santa had said. "That's exactly it." The forge fire cast everything in gold. The workshop smelled like possibility.

He blinked. Stood in his lair again. Cold stone. Bare walls. The warmth was already fading from his chest.

"No, wait," he said, less cheerfully now. "I wasn't done. I need to—"

The last of the curse lifted.

Krampus stood in the middle of his lair, his face falling back into its familiar lines. The weight settled back onto his shoulders—five hundred years of it, all at once.

He looked at his hand. The one that had almost touched the soul's shoulder. The one that had scratched Yule's ears without hesitation. The one that used to reach out to help and had forgotten how.

Slowly, he walked to his chair. Sat down. The silence was absolute.

Every bird watched him. Even Brenda's ongoing conversation with the calling bird had paused.

Krampus sat there, hands on his knees, staring at nothing.

The lost soul's tears. The relief in their voice. The way they'd looked at him like he'd given them something precious.

I've been lost for so long and everyone just walked past.

He remembered that version of himself. The one who stopped. The one who cared about more than just efficiency and punishment. The one who'd believed that even the lost deserved kindness.

When had he stopped being that? The curse hadn't made him fake. It had just removed the armor.

Everything he'd said, everything he'd done— scratching the cat's ears without hesitation, offering genuine help, *caring*—that was still in there somewhere. Buried under centuries of disappointment and isolation and the belief that caring was a weakness he couldn't afford.

But it was still there.

His hand came up, pressed against his chest where something tight and painful was lodging itself.

Yule jumped into his lap. Krampus looked down. The cat looked up.

Those amber eyes saw everything. Had witnessed the whole thing. Knew that something had shifted, some crack had formed in the foundation that Krampus had built his entire existence on.

"Don't look at me like that," Krampus said quietly.

Yule slow-blinked. Then he settled into his lap and started purring.

Krampus sat there, hand hovering over the cat's back, that same half-second of hesitation that always preceded touch.

Then his hand lowered. He sank into the fur. Started stroking.

The birds remained silent. Even the partridge, who always had commentary, said nothing. The doves watched with something like understanding.

The French hens had clustered together on the pear tree, heads tilted in that way that suggested they were bearing witness to something important.

The calling birds had stopped calling.

Krampus pet the cat.

Yule purred.

And in the silence, Krampus tried not to think about how much easier it had been to smile when the curse removed the weight. How much lighter he'd felt. How much he'd enjoyed helping that lost soul find their way.

How much he missed being the person who did that without needing magic to make it possible.

The golden rings lay scattered on his bed, still glowing softly. He didn't touch them again. He didn't need to. The damage—or maybe the revelation—was already done.

Outside, the snow fell upward. The bells rang. His shadow moved independently.

And Krampus sat in his chair, petting a cat whose name he refused to speak, surrounded by birds who saw too much, and tried to remember when armor had stopped being protection and started being a prison.

Yule purred.

His hand kept moving through the soft fur. And for once, he didn't pull away.

THE DEFENSE

The geese arrived like an invading army.

One moment, Krampus was attempting to reorganize his files—still scattered from the cat's first day, made worse by the calling birds' phone chaos, now coated in a fine layer of glitter from a golden ring he'd accidentally brushed against— and the next, there were six enormous geese standing in his lair.

Not standing peacefully. They stood with wings spread, necks extended, eyes gleaming with immediate and inexplicable hostility. The largest one hissed.

"Oh no," the partridge said from its branch.

The goose charged.

Krampus barely dodged as the bird barreled past him, honking with the rage of something that had woken up and chosen violence. It skidded to a halt, turned, and charged again.

"What did I—"

The second goose joined the assault. Then the third. Within seconds, all six were advancing with the coordinated aggression of a tactical strike team.

One of them squatted. Laid an egg.

The egg rolled toward Krampus's foot. Started glowing.

"Run," the partridge said.

"What?"

"RUN!"

Krampus ran.

The egg exploded. Not with fire, but with *glitter*. A detonation of sparkles filled the air with shimmering particles, coating everything within a ten-foot radius. The force of it knocked him forward. He stumbled, caught himself on the filing cabinet, and looked back—

Five more geese were squatting. Five more eggs appeared. All of them glowing.

"OUT!" Vivienne shrieked. "EVERYBODY OUT!"

The birds took flight—partridge, doves, hens, and calling birds all fleeing toward the rafters as Krampus sprinted for the door.

He made it outside just as the eggs detonated in sequence.

BOOM. BOOM. BOOM. BOOM. BOOM.

Glitter exploded through the lair like shrapnel. Gold, silver, red, green, blue—coating every surface, filling the air with a sparkling fog.

The geese emerged from the cloud, honking triumphantly, and immediately spotted him. Charged.

Krampus ran. Not a strategic retreat. Not a tactical withdrawal. Full, undignified fleeing across the alpine landscape while six hostile geese chased him with murderous intent, laying explosive eggs at intervals like the world's most festive minefield.

An egg rolled past him down the slope. Exploded. He was hit with a wave of purple glitter. It went everywhere—in his eyes, his mouth, coating his fur and horns.

"WHAT DID I DO TO YOU?" he shouted at the geese.

They answered by laying more eggs.

He ran faster.

The terrain grew rougher. Snow and rock and treacherous footing. The geese had no such problems, flying short distances to close the gap whenever he got too far ahead.

One landed directly on his head. Started pecking.

Krampus grabbed it and threw it off. The goose flew back, honking outrage, and dive-bombed him with its friends.

He slipped. Went down hard. Rolled. He came to a stop at the base of a pine tree, covered in snow and glitter, breathing hard, with six geese advancing in a semicircle.

They all squatted simultaneously. Six eggs appeared. Started glowing.

"I survived five hundred years," Krampus panted, "for this. Killed by festive poultry."

The eggs glowed brighter.

A black blur shot out from behind the tree.

Yule.

The cat launched himself at the nearest goose with all claws extended, yowling like a demon. The goose honked in surprise. They collided mid-air in an explosion of feathers and fur.

The other geese turned to face this new threat.

Yule landed, puffed up to twice his normal size, and hissed.

The geese hissed back. They stood their ground.

For three long seconds, cat and geese stared at each other.

Then Yule did something unexpected.

He sat down. Slow-blinked at the largest goose. The goose tilted its head. Yule made a small chirping sound—not aggressive, but questioning. The goose's wings lowered slightly.

Yule stood, walked forward with deliberate slowness, and sat down directly in front of the meanest goose. The one that had started the whole chase. He made another chirping sound. The goose honked. Not aggressive. Almost... conversational.

Yule responded with a meow. The goose honked again, softer. They were communicating.

Krampus, still sprawled on the ground and covered in snow, glitter, and pine needles, watched as his cat—his cat, when had that happened?—somehow negotiated with a goose that had just tried to murder him with sparkle bombs.

Yule turned and walked to the second-meanest goose. Sat. Chirped. The goose honked. They touched beaks.

One by one, Yule approached each goose. Sat. Made sounds. Received honks in return. Some kind of understanding passed between them, mediated by a cat who apparently spoke goose.

After the sixth goose, Yule turned and walked back to Krampus. He sat down beside him. Looked at the geese. Meowed once.

The geese waddled forward. Not charging. Just... approaching. They formed a loose circle around Krampus and Yule, then settled onto the snow. Tucked their heads under their wings. Went to sleep.

Just like that. The crisis was over.

Krampus stared at his cat. Yule stared back.

"You..." Krampus started, his throat tight. "You defended me."

Yule slow-blinked.

"You didn't have to. You could have stayed safe in the lair. But you came out here and you—" He stopped. Couldn't finish.

Something was happening in his chest. Something painful and warm and completely unwelcome.

Yule stood, walked closer, and headbutted his hand.

Krampus's fingers curled into the fur automatically.

"...Thanks," he said quietly.

Yule purred.

He rubbed against Krampus's side, coating himself in glitter and snow, clearly not caring.

They sat there in the alpine snow, surrounded by sleeping geese, both of them sparkling like decorations.

It was a moment—the kind that meant something, even if Krampus wasn't ready to name what.

Yule had chosen to protect him. Had put himself between Krampus and danger. Had somehow, impossibly, negotiated peace with hostile poultry through sheer force of cat.

No one had done that for Krampus in… how long? Had anyone ever done that?

His hand tightened in the fur. Yule purred louder.

One of the geese woke up, blinked at them, and did something unprecedented. It squatted. Laid an egg. The egg didn't glow. Didn't explode. It just sat there in the snow. A normal, non-weaponized egg.

"Progress," Krampus muttered.

Yule meowed in agreement.

The goose tucked its head back under its wing.

Krampus looked down at the cat pressed against his side, purring like a small engine, covered in glitter that caught the light.

"You're ridiculous," he said.

Yule's purr intensified.

"Absolutely ridiculous. Defending me from geese. Negotiating truces. Acting like you—"

Like you care. He didn't say it. Couldn't say it. But Yule's slow blink suggested the cat knew anyway.

They sat there until Krampus's legs went numb from the cold, until the glitter started freezing in his fur, until the geese woke up and began waddling back toward the lair in a peaceful formation, apparently having decided he was acceptable now.

When he finally stood, his body protesting every movement, Yule jumped onto his shoulder —the now-familiar weight, the now-familiar purr.

Krampus carried him back to the lair.

The birds were waiting on various perches, covered in glitter themselves.

"Well," the partridge said. "That was educational."

"The chaos agent," Vivienne observed, "has protective instincts. *Intéressant.*"

"He brokered a peace treaty," the first dove added. "With geese. Using only meows and body language."

"Remarkable," the second dove said.

Krampus set Yule down on the guest chair. The cat immediately began grooming glitter out of his fur, completely unconcerned with the birds' commentary.

The geese filed back into the lair, found various corners, and settled down. One was already sitting on its non-explosive egg like it was precious.

"They're staying?" Krampus asked.

"*Bien sûr*," Colette said. "The cat made promises on your behalf."

"What kind of promises?"

"Safety. Shelter. Basic hospitality."

"I didn't agree to—"

The meanest goose looked at him. Honked once. It wasn't a threat. It was a reminder.

Krampus sighed. "Fine. They can stay."

Yule purred from the chair, still grooming, having somehow expanded his domain to include geese diplomacy.

Krampus looked around his lair. The birds in the rafters. The geese in the corners. The pear tree growing through his destroyed table. The scattered files now coated in glitter. Yule grooming on the guest chair that hadn't been used in years until a week ago.

Everything was chaos. Everything was wrong. Everything was...

He stopped that thought. He went to make coffee instead. Found Yule had somehow materialized on the counter, watching him with those knowing amber eyes.

"You're trouble," Krampus said.

Yule headbutted his hand.

"Complete trouble."

Purr.

"But you..." He paused. "...Thank you. For earlier. For defending me."

Yule slow-blinked. Then knocked his coffee

mug off the counter. It shattered. The one he'd used for seventy years. Gone.

Krampus stared at the pieces. He looked at Yule, who was now grooming his paw with supreme indifference.

"Was that necessary?"

Yule meowed.

From the pear tree, Vivienne called out: "He's teaching you about attachment to material objects!"

"He's being a menace!"

"*Peut-être les deux*," Colette suggested. "Perhaps both."

Krampus grabbed a new mug from the cabinet. This one had been a gift from... he couldn't remember. Decades ago. Centuries, maybe.

The coffee was cold anyway. He drank it.

Yule purred from the counter.

The geese slept.

The birds watched.

And Krampus tried not to think about the fact that a cat had defended him from hostile poultry, and that it had meant something.

Outside, the snow fell upward. The bells rang. His shadow moved independently.

And in the corner, covered in glitter, a goose sat on a normal egg like it was a miracle.

Progress.

Chapter Ten

THE TRUTH

Krampus discovered them when he went to wash the glitter off.

It had been three hours since the goose incident. Three hours of finding sparkles in places sparkles had no business being. He'd given up trying to get it out of his fur and decided a bath was the only solution.

He opened the door to his bathroom. Stopped.

Seven swans filled his bathtub. His ONLY bathtub.

They weren't small. They were full-sized, magnificent birds with pure white plumage and long, graceful necks. Somehow, impossibly, all seven of them were floating in the tub as if it were a lake, moving in perfect synchronization. The water sparkled with residual glitter. Gold and silver particles floated on the surface, catching the light.

They turned to look at him in unison.

"Hello, Krampus," they said together, their voices overlapping into eerie harmony.

"No," Krampus said.

"We've been expecting you," the swans continued, still speaking as one. Then the first swan broke from the unified voice.

"Though we must note that the conditions are... suboptimal."

"How is one to reflect on deep truths," the second swan added, ruffling its feathers disdainfully, "in water so full of... *sparkle*?"

"Get out of my bathtub."

"We need to talk about your emotional state," the third swan interjected.

"OUT."

The swans began swimming in a circle. Perfectly synchronized. Hypnotic. Their movements created ripples that somehow looked choreographed.

"Sit down, Krampus," they said.

"I'm not sitting down. I'm not talking to you. I'm—"

"Sitting down," the swans repeated, and somehow the weight of their unified voice made his legs fold.

He sat on the edge of the tub.

The swans continued their circular swimming, necks moving in waves like some kind of aquatic therapy session.

"Let's begin with the obvious," the first swan said, breaking from the unified voice. The others continued swimming silently.

"Your isolation," the second swan added.

"Your resentment," said the third.

"Your burnout," the fourth contributed.

"Your refusal to acknowledge pain," the fifth observed.

"Your substitution of efficiency for meaning," the sixth noted.

"Your anger," the seventh finished.

They all turned to look at him again, still swimming in perfect circles.

"I'm not angry," Krampus said.

All seven swans tilted their heads in identical increments.

"You're furious," the first swan corrected gently. "You've been furious for centuries. But not at who you think."

"I'm not—"

"You blame Santa," the second swan interrupted. "For going soft. For the rebrand. For caring about image."

"He did—"

"But you're not angry at Santa," the third swan said. "You're angry at yourself."

The words hit like a physical blow.

Krampus's hands gripped the edge of the tub.

"That's not—"

"You've been angry since the Plague," the fourth swan continued, still swimming in that hypnotic circle. "Since you took one week—one single week—and the world fell apart. Since you decided it was all your fault."

"It wasn't—"

"You let Santa's doubt become your shame," the fifth swan said. "You saw that flicker in his eyes and turned it inward. Made it a mirror instead of a moment."

"You stopped trying," the sixth swan added. "You stopped believing your work mattered."

"My work does matter—"

"Does it?" the seventh swan asked. "Or have you been going through motions for so long that you've forgotten why you started?"

"I know why I—"

"You've been running on resentment for three centuries," the first swan observed, completing the circle. "Resentment at mortals for not appreciating your efforts. Resentment at Santa for succeeding where you stagnated. Resentment at yourself for becoming this."

The second swan stopped swimming. The others followed suit, all of them facing him now.

"When did duty become suffering?" it asked quietly.

Silence.

The bathroom was too small for this conversation. Too intimate. Water dripped from the faucet. The swans waited.

Krampus's jaw clenched. "I do my job."

"You perform your job," the first swan corrected. "You execute tasks. You maintain systems. But when did you last feel like your work meant something?"

Day Five. The lost soul. The way they'd cried with relief when he'd helped them find their way.

That had felt like something.

"You chose isolation," the second swan said,

"because connection hurt. Because Santa moved on and you felt left behind. Because it was easier to be alone than to risk caring again."

"I didn't—"

"You did," the third swan said. Not unkindly. Just factual. "You made it about efficiency and duty and professional distance because those things can't reject you. Can't leave. Can't change."

"You built a fortress," the fourth swan added, "and called it preference."

"You built a prison," the fifth swan corrected, "and called it choice."

Krampus stood abruptly. "Get out."

The swans didn't move.

"You're angry," the sixth swan observed, "because we're right."

"GET. OUT."

"You're not angry at us," the seventh swan said softly. "You're angry that you spent three hundred years convinced you'd made peace with this life, and a single week with a cat proved you hadn't."

His hands were shaking.

"OUT!"

He grabbed the nearest swan—grabbed it with enough force that he should have hurt it but somehow didn't—and tried to haul it out of the tub.

The swan went limp in his grip, completely unbothered.

"You can remove us," it said calmly. "The truth remains."

Krampus threw it toward the door. It landed gracefully, shook water from its feathers, and waddled toward the exit.

He grabbed the next swan. And the next. One by one, hauling them out of the tub and throwing them toward the door with increasing desperation.

They went without resistance, speaking as they were removed:

"When did you stop believing change was possible?"

"When did duty become your excuse for not living?"

"When did you decide you deserved this loneliness?"

The last swan, he grabbed with both hands and physically carried to the door. It looked at him with dark, knowing eyes.

"The cat sees who you could be," it said. "That's why you're afraid."

He shoved it out and slammed the door.

The silence that followed was absolute. Krampus stood with his back against the door, breathing hard. The words echoed in his head.

You're angry at yourself.

You stopped believing your work mattered.

Running on resentment for three centuries.

When did duty become suffering?

His legs gave out. He slid down the door until he was sitting on the floor.

The bathroom was still wet. Water from the swans dripped from the tiles. The tub was empty now, drain open, water spiraling down in a vortex.

He stared at nothing.

The swans were wrong. They had to be wrong. He'd made peace with this life. He'd chosen it. Chosen the isolation and the efficiency and the distance because it was safer. Because it was—

Because it was easier than admitting he was lonely. Because it was easier than admitting he missed when his work had felt like it mattered. Because it was easier than admitting that watching Santa succeed while he stagnated had broken something in him that he'd never fixed.

Three hundred years. He'd been angry for three hundred years and convinced himself it was principle.

His hands covered his face.

The bathroom door opened.

He didn't look up. Didn't have the energy.

Water sloshed. A splash. A very undignified swan honk.

He looked up.

Yule was sitting on the edge of the tub, one paw still extended from where he'd just pushed a swan into the drain vortex.

The swan was spinning in circles, flapping frantically, honking outrage.

"EMOTIONAL MANIPULATION HAS CONSEQUENCES!" it shrieked as it spiraled toward the drain. "UNRESOLVED TRAUMA CANNOT BE PUSHED AWAY SO EASILY! YOU NEED TO PROCESS YOUR—"

SHLORP

The swan got sucked into the drain that was definitely too small for a swan but apparently operated on dream logic.

Its voice faded to nothing. Silence returned.

Yule sat on the tub edge, grooming his paw with complete satisfaction.

Krampus stared at his cat. His cat who had just committed swan-icide via drain. His cat who had, impossibly, created blessed chaos at exactly the moment he needed it.

"Thank you," Krampus said quietly.

Yule stopped grooming. Looked at him. Slow-blinked. Then jumped down from the tub, walked over, and headbutted his knee.

Krampus's hand came down automatically, burying itself in the soft fur.

They sat there on the bathroom floor—demon and cat, both covered in glitter, surrounded by puddles and the lingering weight of words that couldn't be unsaid.

Eventually, Krampus stood. Gave up on the bath. Went to bed still covered in sparkles.

The lair was quiet.

The birds had settled for the night—partridge in the pear tree, doves on upper branches, hens in a cluster, calling birds silent for once, geese in their corners.

Even the bells had stopped ringing.

Krampus lay in bed, staring at the ceiling, counting cracks he'd memorized centuries ago.

The swans' words played on repeat.

When did duty become suffering?

He didn't have an answer. Or maybe he did, and didn't want to face it.

Weight landed on his chest. He lifted his head slightly. Yule stood there, kneading the blanket, purring already.

"I'm trying to sleep," Krampus said.

Yule circled once. Twice. Then settled directly on his chest, a warm, purring weight pressing down on his sternum.

"This isn't—"

Yule's purr intensified.

Krampus opened his mouth to protest. Closed it. His hand came up. Hovered for half a second. Then lowered to rest on Yule's back.

The purr vibrated through his palm, up his arm, into his chest. The weight was solid. Real. Warm in a way nothing in his lair had been warm in years.

Yule's breathing evened out, slowing into sleep rhythm.

Krampus's hand stayed where it was. Rose and fell with the cat's breathing.

His own breathing began to match it. Slow. Even. Deeper than it had been in—how long?

The tightness in his chest loosened slightly. Not gone. Not fixed. But... less.

Yule's warmth seeped into him. The purr filled the silence that usually pressed down like a physical weight.

For the first time in days—maybe years—maybe centuries—Krampus felt something that might have been peace.

His fingers curled gently in the fur.

Yule purred.

Outside, the snow still fell upward. The bells were quiet. His shadow rested.

And Krampus lay there with a cat sleeping on his chest, his hand rising and falling with each breath, and let himself have this one moment.

Just this one. Tomorrow he could go back to pretending it didn't matter. Tonight, he just... let it be.

His eyes closed.

The purr continued.

The weight on his chest felt like an anchor.

And for the first time in three hundred years, Krampus fell asleep without counting all the ways he was alone.

Chapter Eleven

THE UNEARTHING

The maids materialized at dawn with the energy of people who had a schedule and, by God, they were going to keep it.

Eight of them. Translucent figures in old-fashioned uniforms, carrying buckets, mops, and an alarming array of cleaning supplies that glowed with supernatural efficiency.

The first maid surveyed the lair with the critical eye of someone who had seen worse but was not impressed.

"Goodness," she said.

"Indeed," agreed the second.

"Where do we even begin?" asked the third.

"Everywhere," the first maid decided. "We start everywhere."

They moved as one. What followed was a cleaning blitzkrieg that would have impressed military strategists.

One maid attacked the glitter with a specialized cloth that seemed to absorb sparkles on contact. Another tackled the pear tree, pruning branches with precision shears while leaving the structure intact. A third descended on the filing cabinets with the focused intensity of someone reorganizing a disaster zone.

"Wait," Krampus said, still groggy from the first decent sleep he had enjoyed in years. "Those are organized by—"

"Region and severity, yes," the maid said without looking up. "But the color scheme is all wrong. Look at this—you have red files next to orange files. The chromatic dissonance is distressing."

"It's color-coded for function, not aesthetics—"

"We're fixing it."

She pulled out the entire drawer's contents and began sorting them into piles based on color harmony.

"NO. Those need to stay—"

Another maid was in his workshop, reorganizing the torture implements.

"These chains," she called out, "are lovely! But they would look so much better arranged by metal type. See? Bronze with bronze, iron with iron, and these silver ones—oh, these are exquisite—they should be featured prominently."

She hung them on the wall in an artful display that looked less like a chamber of punishment and more like an avant-garde sculpture installation.

"Those are tools, not decorations!"

"They can be both," the maid said serenely,

stepping back to admire her work. "Beauty and function need not be mutually exclusive."

A third maid had found his kitchen and was reorganizing it with terrifying efficiency. Pots by size. Utensils by frequency of use. Spices alphabetized.

"I had those arranged by—"

"By nothing," the maid interrupted gently. "You had them arranged by nothing. This is better."

She was right. He hated that she was right.

Krampus gave up trying to stop them. He sat down at his desk—which a maid was currently dusting around him without breaking stride— and watched the organized chaos unfold.

Yule emerged from the bedroom, took one look at the maids, and immediately tried to climb the curtains to escape.

A maid caught him mid-climb.

"Oh!" she exclaimed. "What a delightful creature!"

Yule yowled.

"So fluffy! So dark! So perfectly suited to a festive outfit!"

"Don't you dare—" Krampus started.

Too late. From seemingly nowhere, the maid produced a sweater. Red and green with white snowflakes. With a tiny hood. She wrestled it onto Yule with the practiced efficiency of someone who had dressed many unwilling cats.

Yule went rigid. His eyes conveyed betrayal on a cosmic scale. Then, slowly, he looked down at himself. At the sweater. At the tiny hood. Something shifted in his posture.

He jumped down from the maid's arms, landed gracefully, and began walking across the room with deliberate, measured steps. Not slinking. Not skulking. Strutting. Like a runway model. Head high. Tail up. Each paw placed with dramatic precision.

"Oh my," one of the French hens breathed. "He's *serving*."

Yule paused. Posed. One paw raised. Head tilted just so.

The maids applauded.

"Magnificent!" one declared.

"Such presence!" agreed another.

Yule continued his strut, reaching the pear tree, circling it once, then striking another pose.

"You look ridiculous," Krampus said.

Yule turned his head slowly, made direct eye contact, and *strutted* directly toward him. He jumped onto the desk. Posed again, this time with the festive sweater on full display, the tiny snowflakes catching the light.

Krampus's mouth twitched. Almost smiled. Stopped himself. But the corners of his mouth had definitely moved upward for half a second.

Yule saw it. Meowed triumphantly. Strutted away to pose for the geese, who honked their approval.

"That cat," Vivienne observed, "understands drama."

"That cat understands he looks absurd and is

making it everyone else's problem," Krampus muttered.

But he was still watching, still tracking Yule's exaggerated movements around the lair, still fighting that smile.

The maids continued their work, unbothered by the cat fashion show happening around them.

One of them ventured into the storage room—the one Krampus kept locked, the one filled with things from previous centuries that he never looked at because looking meant remembering.

"Oh my!" she called out. "There are such lovely things back here!"

Krampus's head snapped up. "Don't touch—"

She emerged carrying a box.

His heart stopped.

The letter. She found the letter.

Three weeks after the inquiry. Santa's handwriting. The envelope he had shoved deep into that drawer and never opened because opening it would make everything final, would confirm what he already knew—that the partnership was over, that Santa had moved on, that he was alone.

She turned toward him, and he braced for it. For her sympathetic eyes. For the careful way she would hand it over. For the moment he would have to choose between opening it after 287 years or continuing to hide from the truth.

But it was not an envelope. It was a wooden

box. His handwriting on the side. Old handwriting, from when he had still bothered with decorative script.

The relief lasted half a second before new dread set in. That box. Those decorations. Those memories.

"What beautiful decorations!" the maid said, setting it on the now-pristine desk. "Are these vintage? They're extraordinary!"

"Put those back."

"But they're—"

"Back. Now."

The maid's enthusiasm dimmed slightly. She looked at him, then at the box, then back at him with an expression that suggested she understood more than he wanted her to.

"Of course," she said gently. "I'll just leave this here in case you change your mind."

She returned to her cleaning.

The box sat on his desk. Krampus stared at it. He did not open it. He went back to pretending to work on files that the maids had reorganized into incomprehensible (but aesthetically pleasing) arrangements.

Yule strutted past again, still modeling his sweater, now incorporating spins into his routine.

One of the doves began humming what might have been runway music.

Krampus's hands stilled on the files. His eyes drifted to the box.

It had been there for decades. Maybe a

century. He had locked it away after the last time he had looked inside, after the last time the memories had hurt too much to bear.

His hand reached out. Stopped. Reached again. He opened the lid.

The smell hit him first. Old paper. Dried pine. Something that might have been cinnamon from a pomander ball that had long since disintegrated.

Inside: decorations. Hand-painted baubles. Garland made from something organic that had crumbled to dust. A string of bells—real ones, not magical—that someone had tied together with red ribbon.

And underneath it all: a photograph.

He pulled it out carefully. The paper was stiff with age, the image faded to sepia tones. Two figures stood in front of what looked like a workshop. One was unmistakably Santa—younger somehow, though immortals do not age, maybe just less burdened. The other was Krampus. Both of them were laughing.

Not smiling for the camera. Actually laughing, caught mid-moment, Santa's hand on Krampus's shoulder, Krampus's head thrown back, both of them looking as if they had just shared the funniest joke in the world.

The memory surfaced with startling clarity.

The sharp, clean scent of winter air. The distant ring of elven hammers singing against metal in the workshop yards. And Santa's laugh—that deep, rumbling warmth beside him that had felt like safety.

Like coming home. The kind of sound you did not think about until it was gone, and then you could not remember how you had ever breathed without it.

Krampus did not remember what the joke had been. He could not remember the last time he had laughed like that. He could not remember when Santa's hand on his shoulder had stopped feeling natural and started feeling like something he had lost—something he had given away and could never get back.

His throat closed up. Beneath the photo: the ornament. The same one from the locked drawer in the filing cabinet. The hand-carved one with both their initials intertwined.

K & S.

Someone had made it for them. He could not remember who. Some spirit or elf or grateful soul who had seen them working together and wanted to commemorate it.

Partnership, the design said. *Unity. Two parts of one whole.*

"Oh, how lovely!" one of the maids said, appearing at his shoulder.

Krampus quickly set the photo face-down.

"Should we put these up?" the maid continued, gesturing at the decorations in the box. "They're beautiful. And this ornament—it's clearly special. It should be displayed, don't you think?"

"No," Krampus said. Too quick. Too sharp.

The maid's expression softened. "Of course. Your lair, your choice."

She moved away to organize something else.

Krampus sat there, the ornament in his hand. He should put it back in the box. Back in storage. Back in the locked room where it could not make him remember things that only hurt.

His hand placed it on the desk instead. Front and center, where he would see it every time he looked up. The photo, he tucked back into the box.

Looking at that—at them laughing, at Santa's hand on his shoulder, at whatever version of himself had existed before the isolation calcified—that was too much.

But the ornament... He could keep the ornament out. Just this once. Just for now.

"Looking good!" a maid called to Yule, who was now posing on top of the filing cabinet, sweater fully displayed, tail raised like a flag.

Yule meowed and struck another pose.

Krampus's gaze drifted from the cat to the ornament.

K & S.

When had they stopped being that? A unified partnership? When had it become separate territories, formal quarterly reviews, communication through HR instead of just... talking?

His finger traced the carved letters.

"I see you admiring our work on the cat," one of the maids said, startling him.

His hand jerked away from the ornament. "I was not—"

"The sweater really brings out his eyes, don't you think?"

Krampus looked at Yule, who was now attempting to incorporate the pear tree into his routine, weaving between branches like he was on an obstacle course runway.

"He looks absurd," Krampus said.

But his eyes were soft when he said it. And he was definitely almost smiling.

The maid noticed. She smiled herself. Said nothing. She just went back to organizing his torture implements by aesthetic coherence.

By midday, the lair was transformed. Not fundamentally different. Still stone. Still dark. Still his. But it was cleaner. More organized. With small touches of beauty woven in where function used to rule alone.

The chains were arranged artfully. The files were color-coordinated. The kitchen was actually functional. Even the pear tree had been pruned into something that looked intentional rather than chaotic.

And on his desk: the ornament. Catching the light. Impossible to ignore.

The maids gathered by the door, preparing to leave.

"We'll check in periodically," the first maid said. "To maintain our work. But honestly, you just need to dust regularly. And perhaps consider adding some warmth to the space. Some color. Some life."

She glanced meaningfully at Yule, still in his

sweater, now grooming himself on the guest chair.

"The cat helps," she added.

They vanished in a shimmer of light.

The lair was quiet again.

Krampus looked around at the reorganized chaos.

At Yule, still wearing the ridiculous sweater, now asleep on the chair.

At the ornament on his desk.

He picked it up. Turned it over in his hands.

K & S.

Someone had made this when they had still been a team. When the work had been about balance, not territory. When connection had felt natural instead of dangerous.

His thumb traced the letters. He set it back down. He did not put it away. He went back to work instead, files now organized by incomprehensible color schemes, but somehow he did not mind as much as he thought he would.

Every time he looked up, the ornament was there. A reminder of what had been. Maybe a reminder of what could be again, if he could figure out how to unbuild three hundred years of walls.

Yule stretched in his sleep, the festive sweater riding up slightly.

Krampus watched him. His mouth twitched. Almost smiled. This time, he let it.

THE DANCE

The ladies arrived in a whirl of silk and bells.

Nine of them. Tall, graceful, dressed in gowns that seemed to be made of music itself—fabric that shimmered and flowed and somehow chimed softly with every movement.

They took one look at Krampus's living area —the space between his desk and the pear tree, what remained of his sitting room—and declared it a dance floor.

"Perfect!" the first lady said, clapping her hands.

"Absolutely perfect!" the second agreed.

"Wonderful spacing!" added the third.

Before Krampus could protest, they'd formed a circle and begun dancing.

Not normal dancing. This was choreographed performance art. They moved as one entity, spinning and stepping and twirling with synchronized precision. Their feet made no sound on the stone floor, but the bells in their clothing created a constant, hypnotic rhythm.

"Excuse me," Krampus said.

They didn't stop. He tried to walk to his desk. The moment he entered the circle, a lady grabbed his hand.

"No, I don't—"

She pulled him into the formation. Another lady took his other hand. Within seconds, he was part of the circle, being swept along in movements his body didn't know.

"I'm not dancing—"

"One-two-three, one-two-three," the ladies chanted, guiding his feet through a waltz pattern.

"This is ridiculous—"

"Step, pivot, turn!"

His body followed despite himself. Muscle memory from centuries ago—from festivals he'd attended when the work had still been new, when celebration had been part of the rhythm of the year instead of something other people did.

"I need to—"

"Excellent! Now spin!"

She spun him. The room whirled past—pear tree, filing cabinets, watching birds, Yule sitting on the desk in his festive sweater.

He stumbled slightly on the dismount. The lady caught him smoothly, transitioned into a different dance.

"I really should—"

"Box step! You remember box steps?"

His feet did, apparently.

"This is unnecessary—"

"Now dip!"

She dipped him backward. He was supporting her weight, his arm automatically going around her waist, his other hand holding hers in the proper position.

When had he last danced? Before the isolation. Before the burnout. Before he'd decided that joy was a frivolous distraction from duty.

The lady pulled him upright and immediately handed him off to another.

"My turn!" the new partner declared, and swept him into what might have been a foxtrot.

"I'm trying to work—"

"Work later! Dance now!"

His mouth opened to protest. A laugh came out instead. Not a dark chuckle. Not a sarcastic bark. An actual laugh, surprised and genuine and completely unbidden.

The lady grinned. "There it is!"

"I didn't mean to—"

Then they arrived.

Ten lords materialized mid-waltz in a cascade of silk and arrogance. Tall, impossibly beautiful fae nobility dressed in jewel-toned coats—emerald, sapphire, ruby, amethyst—that caught the light with every motion.

The first lord appeared on top of the filing cabinet, looked down at the floor, and sneered.

"Walking," he announced, "is for *peasants*."

Then he leaped. A supernatural bound that carried him directly through the circle of dancers. A lady spun Krampus out of the way at the last second—perfectly timed, incorporating the dodge into the choreography.

The lord landed on the pear tree's highest branch.

"Quite right!" the second lord agreed, materializing on the guest chair. "One simply doesn't *walk* when one can *leap*!"

He launched himself toward a ceiling beam, using a dancing lady's shoulder as a springboard mid-leap.

She didn't miss a beat, just adjusted her spin to account for the weight, pulling Krampus with her through a turn that barely avoided a third lord bounding past.

"The aesthetic of the leap," the third lord declared, materializing directly in the center of the dance floor, "is vastly superior to pedestrian ambulation!"

The ladies danced around him without breaking formation.

He sprang at the fourth lord, who was leaping from the kitchen counter.

Mid-leap, his foot hit something slick. A non-explosive goose egg, rolled into a corner and forgotten from days ago. His trajectory went sideways.

They collided mid-air above Krampus's head—not gracefully, but in a flailing tangle of limbs. Pinballed off each other. Fell toward him.

A lady grabbed Krampus's hand and yanked him into a dramatic dip just as both lords crashed into the space where he'd been standing.

"Excellent reflexes!" she said cheerfully, pulling him back upright and spinning him directly into the path of another leaping lord.

"I can't—there are too many—"

"Just follow my lead!"

She spun him under her arm. A lord sailed overhead, using the momentum to bounce off the wall.

"This is—"

"Dancing! And dodging! Multi-tasking!"

The fifth lord leaped between them, separating their joined hands. Another lady caught Krampus immediately, swept him into a new pattern.

"Watch out for the—"

A lord landed on his shoulder, used it as a springboard, and launched toward the chandelier Krampus didn't have.

"—lords," Krampus finished, stumbling.

The lady steadied him, incorporated his stumble into a spin. Around them, complete chaos.

Lords bounding off every surface—the filing cabinets, the pear tree, the dancing ladies themselves who had somehow transformed their choreography into an obstacle course. The ladies spun and dipped and twirled, pulling Krampus through the formation while lords ricocheted overhead, beside, through them.

A lord landed on another lord mid-leap.

"Stack formation!" one declared.

They crashed into a dancing lady. She caught

them, used their momentum to execute a lift, and tossed them toward the ceiling.

"Magnificent!" the sixth lord called from his perch on the pear tree. "Peasant-tier execution, but magnificent!"

He leaped at the partridge, who ducked. The lord hit the trunk, slid down dramatically.

"My dignity," he moaned.

A dancing lady swept past, grabbed his hand, pulled him into the formation.

"No! I don't *dance*! I *leap*!"

"You can do both!" she said cheerfully, spinning him.

He went with it despite himself, his face registering absolute horror.

Krampus was laughing again. Actually laughing, breathless and overwhelmed, as a lady spun him under her arm and two lords bounded overhead in perfect synchronization.

His horns got in the way during one particularly ambitious spin while simultaneously dodging a leaping lord. He had to duck. Nearly collided with both a lady and a lord. Caught himself at the last second.

The lady caught him, the lord bounced off his shoulder, and somehow all three of them ended up in a bizarre, improvised formation that shouldn't have worked but did. The laugh became uncontrollable.

The ladies had fully incorporated the lords into their choreography now. Lords were being used as props, as springboards, as unexpected lifts. One lady would spin, a lord would leap, and somehow they'd meet in perfect timing for a joint maneuver that looked rehearsed but was clearly chaos.

The seventh lord tried to leap onto Krampus's horns.

A dancing lady intercepted him mid-air, used his momentum to execute a dramatic dip with Krampus, then released the lord who pinballed off the filing cabinet—directly into the workshop doorway where the maids had artfully displayed the chains.

He hit the silver ones with a musical *clang*, got tangled in bronze, and ended up hanging upside down wrapped in iron like a very dignified Christmas ornament.

"MY AESTHETIC!" he wailed.

A dancing lady swept past and untangled him without missing a step in her choreography, setting him back on his feet. He immediately leaped again, pretending nothing had happened.

"This is insane!" Krampus said.

"This is *FUN!*" the lady corrected, spinning him directly into another partner.

The eighth and ninth lords were engaged in a leaping competition through the dance formation.

"Nine points!" one declared, sailing over Krampus's head.

"Watch the form!" the other countered, using a lady's shoulders to execute a double bounce.

They collided mid-air. Fell. The dancing

ladies caught them, incorporated them into a group lift, and tossed them at the pear tree.

The geese honked in rhythm with the bells.

The French hens were providing live commentary in French, half sarcastic, half impressed.

The doves had given up taking notes and were just watching with stunned fascination.

The partridge looked like it was reconsidering every life choice.

A chirp cut through the chaos.

Krampus's head snapped toward the sound.

Yule—still in his festive sweater—was crouched on the filing cabinet. Tail swishing. Pupils dilated. Every muscle tensed.

He was hunting. A lady spun Krampus past. A lord leaped overhead. And Yule launched. Not at a lord. Not at a lady. Directly at Krampus's legs, trajectory calculated perfectly to intercept him mid-waltz.

Impact. Krampus's feet tangled with cat. He went down hard, taking a dancing lady with him, who grabbed a lord for balance, who grabbed another lord, who grabbed another lady—

The entire formation collapsed in a domino effect of silk, fur, bells, and limbs. They hit the floor in a heap. For one beat: absolute silence. Then laughter erupted from everyone simultaneously.

The ladies were giggling, bells chiming with every shake of their shoulders. The lords—even the lords—were laughing despite themselves, wounded dignity abandoned in the sheer absurdity. One was still tangled with a dancing lady, another had landed on top of the partridge's branch, a third had somehow ended up wrapped in his own coat.

And Krampus lay at the bottom of the pile, Yule sitting triumphantly on his chest, and he couldn't stop laughing. Not a polite chuckle. Not a dark comment. Pure, uncontrolled, breathless laughter that shook his whole body and filled the lair and bounced off walls that hadn't heard that sound in centuries.

He was having *fun*. The realization hit with physical force. Being pulled into absurd dances while dodging leaping lords. Being tripped by his cat. Lying on the floor of his lair in a pile of magical beings, and it was—

Wonderful. Terrifying. He didn't know what to do with it.

Yule purred louder, kneading his chest, apparently very pleased with himself.

"Did you trip me on purpose?" Krampus asked, still breathless.

Yule's purr intensified.

"Of course you did."

A dancing lady extracted herself from the pile, offered her hand. "One more dance?"

A lord, still tangled with another lady, called out: "One more leap?"

Krampus looked around at the chaos. At the ladies picking themselves up gracefully. At the lords trying to regain dignity while still laughing.

At Yule, purring victoriously. At the birds watching with knowing eyes.

"One more," he heard himself say.

The ladies and lords cheered. They sorted themselves out—ladies reforming their circle, lords finding new perches to leap from. But this time, they were working together. A lady would spin, a lord would leap, and they'd create something that was half dance, half aerial acrobatics, all chaos.

And Krampus was in the center of it. Laughing when he nearly collided with a leaping lord. Gasping when a lady spun him directly under a mid-air lord collision. Actually enjoying the complete, overwhelming, impossible absurdity of dancing in his own lair while ten aristocratic fae used the choreography as a leaping course.

When the music finally paused—the ladies slowing, the lords landing—he was breathing hard. His face hurt from smiling. His chest felt expanded, like something compressed had finally been allowed to unfold.

"Same time tomorrow?" one of the ladies asked.

"Perhaps a leaping demonstration?" a lord suggested, having apparently decided this was acceptable behavior.

"I—" Krampus started.

"Wonderful!" they said in unison.

The ladies continued their dance, slower now, background movement. The lords found perches and settled, occasionally doing small leaps between surfaces but with less aggression.

They'd integrated. Somehow, impossibly, they were coexisting in his lair.

Krampus returned to his desk. Yule jumped into his lap immediately. His hand went to the cat's back automatically.

Around him, lords occasionally leaped while ladies danced. The geese honked. The hens commented. The chaos had become... ambient. Manageable. Even pleasant.

A lord landed on his desk.

"Excellent perch," the lord declared, looking at his files.

Krampus just moved his coffee mug without looking up.

"You're not even reacting anymore," the partridge observed.

Krampus didn't argue.

A lord leaped past. A lady spun through. Yule purred in his lap.

And Krampus sat in the eye of the storm, surrounded by chaos he'd stopped fighting, reading his files and scratching his cat's ears.

He'd adapted. Finally.

Outside, the snow fell upward.

Inside, dancing and leaping continued in strange harmony.

And Krampus, for the first time in centuries, felt like maybe he could breathe.

Chapter Thirteen

THE PRESSURE

The pipers appeared at dusk.

Eleven of them. Dressed in military-style uniforms that might have been from any century between the fifteenth and the twentieth. Each held a pipe—some wooden, some metal, all gleaming with an unsettling sheen.

They stood in formation in the center of the lair. Raised their pipes to their lips. And began to play. The sound was immediate and inescapable.

Not loud. Worse than loud. It was a single, cursed tune that burrowed into the brain and nested there, repeating endlessly, impossible to ignore or tune out.

Three notes. Over and over. A melody that shouldn't have been disturbing but somehow was, like a music box winding down in an empty room.

The pipers didn't stop. Didn't pause for breath. Just piped. Constantly. Within five minutes, the first rat appeared.

It materialized from the shadows near the filing cabinet, drawn by the music. Then another.

Then a dozen more, streaming from cracks in the stone that Krampus didn't remember being there.

They sat in clusters, swaying to the cursed tune.

"Make them stop," Krampus said.

The pipers kept piping. The shadows began moving wrong.

Not his shadow—that had been acting independently for days. All the shadows. Stretching. Reaching. Pulling themselves from walls and corners like they were trying to escape into three dimensions.

One shadow peeled itself entirely from the floor and stood upright, featureless and dark, swaying to the music.

"STOP," Krampus said louder.

The pipers piped. A feeling settled over the lair. Not quite fear. Not quite dread. Something between them—a low-grade anxiety that crawled under the skin and made everything feel slightly wrong.

The rats kept appearing. The shadows kept multiplying. The anxiety intensified with each repetition of the three-note tune.

Krampus tried to work. Couldn't focus. The music drilled into his skull. Tried to read. The words swam on the page. Tried to organize files. Gave up after dropping the same folder three times.

The pipers stood in formation. Played their tune. Never stopped.

The lords tried leaping around them. One landed too close. The piper didn't flinch, just kept playing while a lord used his head as a springboard.

The dancing ladies attempted to incorporate them into choreography. The pipers remained stationary, pipes raised, music unceasing.

The geese honked in protest. The hens complained in French. The doves offered therapeutic observations about anxiety management. The partridge gave up and buried its head under a wing.

The calling birds tried to drown them out by making more calls. Failed. Brenda was trying to describe her pot roast recipe over the piping and losing.

Yule sat on the desk, ears flat, tail lashing. Even the cat looked miserable.

Krampus made it to midnight before he gave up on functioning. Went to bed. Lay there, staring at the ceiling.

The piping continued. Three notes. Over and over. Muffled slightly by the bedroom door but still there, drilling into his brain, making sleep impossible.

The rats scratched in the walls. The shadows moved across the ceiling in patterns that suggested consciousness. The anxiety pressed down like a physical weight.

He closed his eyes. The music played behind his eyelids. Opened them. A shadow stood in the corner of his bedroom, swaying. He rolled over.

More shadows on that wall, all moving to the cursed tune.

One hour passed.

Two.

Three.

The piping never stopped.

By 3 AM, Krampus was staring at nothing, exhausted beyond thought, too tired to sleep, too overwhelmed to function.

The rats had found their way into his bedroom. Dozens of them, sitting on the floor in neat rows, swaying in unison.

The shadows had multiplied. They covered the walls now, peeling away, standing on their own, creating a crowd of darkness that pulsed with the three-note melody.

The anxiety had settled into his bones. Everything felt wrong. Everything felt impossible.

Five hundred and thirty-seven years of holding it together, and he was being broken by eleven musicians and a cursed tune.

A sound at the door. Soft padding. Yule appeared, silhouetted against the dim light from the main room. He was carrying something in his mouth.

Walked carefully across the room, navigating around the swaying rats, through the crowd of animate shadows. Jumped onto the bed. Set down his cargo with gentle precision. The ornament.

K & S.

Yule sat back. Looked at Krampus with those amber eyes. Purred—loud enough to be heard even over the distant piping.

Krampus stared at the cat. At the ornament.

"You're chaos incarnate," he said. His voice was rough from hours of silence. Delirious from exhaustion. "Pure, unfiltered chaos."

Yule's purr intensified.

"You've destroyed my filing system. My furniture. My routine. Every single aspect of my carefully ordered life."

Yule tilted his head.

"You brought me birds. Geese. Lords. Pipers who won't STOP PIPING."

The cat headbutted his hand. The touch grounded him. Warm. Real. Present.

Krampus picked up the ornament with his other hand. Turned it over slowly in the dim light.

K & S.

Someone had carved this. Had seen them working together and thought it worth commemorating. Had believed their partnership mattered enough to make something beautiful about it.

When had it stopped mattering? When had he decided it was safer to be alone than to risk that kind of connection again?

The piping continued in the background. The rats swayed. The shadows moved. The anxiety pressed down.

But Yule was here. Had brought him the one

thing that represented what he'd lost. Was purring in the darkness like it was enough just to be here. Like Krampus was enough.

His thumb traced the intertwined letters.

"Santa sent you," he said quietly. Not a question. A realization he'd been avoiding. "He knew. He knew I was—"

Drowning. Suffocating. Running on empty for so long he'd forgotten what full felt like.

Yule headbutted his hand again.

Krampus set the ornament down carefully on the bedside table. His hand moved to Yule's back, fingers sinking into the soft fur.

The piping played on.

The chaos continued.

But here, in this small space, with a cat purring against his hand and an ornament catching what little light there was, something settled.

"...Fine," Krampus said. "Your name is Yule."

The purr got louder. Impossibly louder.

Yule pressed his head more firmly against Krampus's palm, rubbing with deliberate pressure.

"That's your name. Yule. After the season. After the thing I used to celebrate before I forgot how."

Yule's whole body vibrated with purring.

"Don't let it go to your head."

Yule pulled away from his hand. Looked him directly in the eyes. Reached out one deliberate paw. Knocked a book off the bedside table. It hit the floor with a thud that barely registered over the piping.

Krampus stared at the cat. At the fallen book. At Yule's utterly unrepentant face. A sound escaped him. Not a growl. Not a sigh. A laugh.

Quiet at first, then building. His shoulders shaking. His chest heaving. Sound pouring out of him that didn't care about the piping or the anxiety or the exhaustion.

He was laughing. Actually laughing, delirious and exhausted and completely overwhelmed, but laughing at the sheer audacity of a cat who'd just been named and immediately proved he'd learned nothing from the experience.

Yule purred louder, clearly pleased with himself. Walked in a circle on the bed. Settled down directly on Krampus's chest, still purring like an engine.

The laugh faded to breathless chuckling. Krampus's hand came up automatically, resting on Yule's back.

"You're impossible," he said.

Yule purred.

"Absolutely impossible."

The purr vibrated through his palm, into his chest, somehow managing to exist louder than the piping.

His fingers curled into the fur.

"But you're mine."

The words came out without permission. Hung in the air between them. True in a way that made his throat tight.

Yule's eyes closed slowly. Opened. Slow-blinked in that way cats do when they're content.

Krampus's other hand came up to the cat. Both hands now, cradling the warm weight on his chest.

The piping continued. The rats swayed. The shadows moved. The anxiety pressed down.

But Yule was here. Yule was *his*. And that somehow made it bearable.

"Named after winter solstice," Krampus murmured, exhaustion finally pulling at him. "After the longest night. After the promise that light comes back."

Yule purred.

"Pretentious, probably."

Louder purring.

"But it fits."

His eyes closed.

The piping played on, but it felt further away now. Muffled by the purring on his chest, by the weight of acceptance settling into his bones.

He'd named the cat. Had admitted it was his. Had laughed in the middle of the longest night, surrounded by cursed music and animate shadows. Had chosen, finally, to stop fighting.

His breathing slowed. Matched Yule's rhythm.

The purr vibrated through him like a lullaby that defied the cursed tune trying to burrow into his brain.

He fell asleep with his hands on the cat's back, the ornament on his bedside table catching the shadows' movement, and something in his chest that felt lighter than it had in three hundred years.

The pipers piped. The rats swayed. The shadows danced.

And Krampus slept. Finally.

Morning came too soon.

Krampus woke to find Yule still on his chest, still purring, the pipers still piping their cursed three-note tune.

The rats were everywhere. The shadows had taken over half the lair. The anxiety was a constant hum under everything.

But he'd slept. Somehow, impossibly, with a cat on his chest and acceptance in his heart, he'd slept.

Yule opened his eyes. Slow-blinked.

"Morning, Yule," Krampus said.

The name felt right in his mouth. Felt like something that had always been true, just waiting to be said aloud.

Yule purred. Stood. Stretched elaborately. And knocked the ornament off the bedside table.

Krampus caught it before it hit the floor.

"Really?"

Yule meowed innocently.

"You're doing this on purpose."

Another meow, this one smug.

Krampus looked at the ornament in his hand. At the cat who'd brought it to him in the middle of the night. At the chaos visible through his bedroom door—pipers still playing, shadows still moving, rats still multiplying.

One more day. One more impossible day, and then the final convergence.

He set the ornament back on the table. Stood. Yule jumped to his shoulder, that now-familiar weight.

"Let's go see what fresh hell awaits," Krampus said.

Yule purred agreement.

They walked out together into the piping chaos.

And Krampus found he could face it. With a cat named Yule on his shoulder and the memory of laughter still warm in his chest, he could face anything.

Chapter Fourteen

THE CONVERGENCE

The drummers didn't appear.

They manifested inside Krampus's skull.

One moment he was drinking coffee—cold, always cold now—watching Yule chase a rat through the swaying shadows while the pipers piped their endless tune.

The next moment: *BOOM.*

The sound exploded from inside his head. Not in his ears. In his *brain.* Like someone had set up a full drumline in the space between his thoughts and told them to play as loud as physically possible.

BOOM. BOOM. BOOM.

A rhythm. Twelve drummers, twelve different drums, all pounding in perfect synchronization inside his consciousness.

Krampus dropped his mug. It shattered.

Yule's head snapped up.

BOOM. BOOM. BOOM.

The piping was still there. Three notes, endlessly repeating. But now there were drums underneath, behind, around, *through* the melody.

The rats scattered. The shadows froze mid-sway. Every bird in the lair turned to look at him.

BOOM. BOOM. BOOM.

"What—" Krampus started.

The air began to shimmer. Reality bent.

The drumming intensified—not louder, *deeper*. Each beat resonated through dimensions, triggering something fundamental in the magical structure holding everything together.

Dimensional resonance.

The partridge flew up from its branch, glowing brighter. The doves began circling. The French hens started speaking in rapid, overlapping French. The calling birds' phones all rang at once. The geese honked in alarm. The dancing ladies spun faster. The lords leaped frantically. The pipers piped louder. The maids materialized and began cleaning in double-time.

And the golden rings—sitting forgotten in a drawer—began to glow. Everything was activating. At once.

BOOM. BOOM. BOOM.

The first partridge multiplied. Suddenly there were six of them, all glowing, all offering psychological assessments simultaneously:

"You're avoiding the core issue—"

"—pattern of self-sabotage—"

"—unresolved abandonment trauma—"

"—fear of vulnerability—"

"—thirty-seven documented instances—"

"—WHEN DID JOY BECOME DANGEROUS—"

The turtle doves were suddenly everywhere, circling his head in pairs, offering competing therapeutic frameworks:

"Attachment theory suggests—"

"No, cognitive behavioral—"

"Clearly psychodynamic—"

"Have you considered mindfulness—"

The French hens had unionized. Again. And again. Multiple versions of them, all negotiating different contracts:

"We demand heated coops!"

"Better lighting!"

"Aesthetic coherence!"

"WORKPLACE DIGNITY!"

"*Plus de fromage!*"

The calling birds were making calls. Hundreds of them. Phones ringing from every surface, every dimension, all at once:

Loki: "STOP CALLING ME—"

Derek from USPS: "Sir, I still don't understand the question—"

Brenda: "—and then he reorganized the spice rack WITHOUT TELLING ME—"

Santa: "Krampus? KRAMPUS?!"

The geese were laying eggs. Explosive ones. Constantly. Eggs materialized and detonated in rapid succession—*BOOM*-glitter-*BOOM*-sparkles-*BOOM*-everywhere.

The swans had taken over every water source. The bathtub. A bucket. A puddle. All performing synchronized psychoanalysis:

"You're running from yourself—"

"—been running for centuries—"

"—can't outrun internal conflict—"

"—duty became suffering when—"

The maids were cleaning with supernatural speed, reorganizing everything, finding boxes upon boxes of old memories, pulling them all out:

Photos everywhere. Krampus and Santa through the centuries. Laughing. Working. Side by side. Partners.

Decorations cascading from storage. Ornaments. Garland. Bells. Things he'd locked away because remembering hurt.

The dancing ladies had multiplied into a full chorus line, pulling everything into their choreography. Lords leaping into lifts. Swans incorporated into synchronized swimming-dancing hybrids. Geese as percussion via explosive eggs.

The lords were leaping. Dozens of them. Hundreds. Ricocheting off every surface, off each other, creating impossible trajectories:

"EXCELLENT PERCH—"

"—MY TRAJECTORY—"

"—PEASANT-TIER LEAP—"

"—STACK FORMATION—"

The pipers piped. The cursed tune multiplied into harmony, then discord, then something that sounded like reality breaking.

The rats swarmed. Thousands of them, swaying in perfect unison to the overlapping rhythms.

The shadows pulled themselves free from every surface. Stood. Danced. Moved independently. Became a crowd of darkness that filled every space.

And through it all: *BOOM. BOOM. BOOM.*

The drumming in his skull. Relentless. Inescapable.

Krampus staggered. Put his hands to his head. Everything was happening. All at once.

Every gift. Every day. Every manifestation. Compressed into a single moment that stretched and fractured and multiplied into infinite chaos.

He couldn't process it. Couldn't separate the sounds—piping, drumming, honking, phone ringing, French arguing, therapeutic observations, lords shouting, dancers singing, bells chiming, explosions, purring—

Wait. Purring?

He looked down. Through the chaos. Through the swirling mass of birds and lords and shadows and rats and explosive glitter.

Yule sat in the exact center of the lair. Perfectly still. Perfectly calm. Sitting with his tail wrapped around his paws, wearing his festive sweater, eyes half-closed. Purring.

The sound cut through everything. Louder than the piping. Deeper than the drumming. More present than the chaos. A rumble that seemed to come from the foundation of reality itself.

Yule's eyes opened. Looked directly at Krampus. Glowed. Not reflecting light.

Generating it. Amber becoming gold becoming something that looked like captured starlight.

The purring intensified. The chaos swirled faster.

Partridges offering diagnoses. Doves in therapy circles. Hens negotiating. Birds calling. Geese exploding. Swans psychoanalyzing. Maids organizing memories. Ladies dancing. Lords leaping. Pipers piping. Drummers drumming inside his head.

And through it all, Yule purred. Like a small god. Like the eye of a hurricane. Like something ancient and powerful that had been waiting for this exact moment.

BOOM. BOOM. BOOM.

The drumming crescendoed. The dimensional resonance peaked. Everything converged.

Krampus's knees buckled. Too much. Too loud. Too bright. Too *everything*. He couldn't—

His vision blurred. The lair spun.

Five hundred years of control. Of order. Of carefully maintained distance and isolation and armor.

Falling apart. Everything falling apart. He hit the floor. Hands flat on cold stone. Breathing ragged. The chaos swirled above him. Around him. Through him.

BOOM. BOOM. BOOM.

"I can't—" he gasped.

The partridges: "You're experiencing breakthrough—"

The doves: "This is progress—"

The hens: "*C'est nécessaire!*"

The swans: "Transformation requires destruction of old patterns—"

"STOP," Krampus said. Tried to say. Couldn't hear his own voice over the noise.

BOOM. BOOM. BOOM.

The drumming shook his bones. The piping drilled into his brain. The chaos pressed down from every direction.

He was breaking. Finally, completely breaking. And in the center of it all, Yule sat. Watching. Waiting. Purring like this was exactly what was supposed to happen. Like this was the plan all along.

The lair filled with light. Chaos. Sound. Movement. Memory. Everything he'd tried to bury. Everything he'd tried to control. Everything he'd tried to avoid.

All of it at once. And Krampus knelt in the center of the storm, hands pressed to the floor, breathing shallow, control shattered, walls crumbling, armor destroyed.

Overwhelmed. Completely. Utterly. Overwhelmed.

The chaos peaked. The drumming thundered. Yule purred. And everything—

Chapter Fifteen

THE MELTDOWN

The chaos didn't stop.

Krampus stayed on the floor—hands flat on stone, breath coming in shallow gasps—and the chaos continued around him. Above him. Through him.

The partridges were mid-negotiation with the French hens about jurisdictional boundaries. All six of them. All nine hens. The discussion had devolved into a shouting match about whether psychological assessment fell under "workplace wellness" or constituted "emotional labor requiring additional compensation."

"—CLEARLY STATES IN SUBSECTION 7—"

"—*NON*, THAT ONLY APPLIES TO—"

"—HAZARD PAY—"

"—THERAPEUTIC OVERREACH—"

A goose laid an egg directly next to Krampus's hand. It detonated. Gold glitter coated his fingers. He didn't move them.

The dancing ladies had incorporated the leaping lords into an elaborate aerial ballet. One lord used a swan's back as a springboard. The swan, mid-psychoanalysis, didn't break stride.

"—your resistance to connection stems from —*EXCUSE ME*—fear of abandonment—*COULD YOU NOT*—that manifests as—"

The lord leaped away and landed on a piper. The piper kept piping. The cursed three-note melody wove through the drumming still thundering in Krampus's skull. BOOM-tweet-BOOM-tweet-BOOM-tweet in an endless, maddening rhythm.

The maids had formed an assembly line, passing memories from the storage room to various display locations.

A photo of Krampus and Santa building the first naughty list together.

A carved wooden sign: "PARTNERSHIP HEADQUARTERS."

Letters. Dozens of them. Correspondence spanning centuries, starting warm, growing formal, eventually stopping altogether.

The last one, dated 287 years ago. *I miss working with you. Can we talk?*

Unopened. Still unopened.

A maid set it on the floor near Krampus's hand. He stared at it. Didn't pick it up.

The calling birds had established a full switchboard operation. Phones rang constantly.

"—LOKI SAYS TO STOP CALLING—"

"—Derek wants to know about holiday shipping rates—"

"—Brenda is concerned about your well-being—"

"—SANTA ON LINE THREE—"

"—MYTHIC TELECOMMUNICATIONS BUREAU, PLEASE HOLD—"

The rats had formed organized groups by species, swaying in synchronized patterns to the competing rhythms, creating waves of rodent choreography. The shadows had become a crowd. Hundreds, thousands, all moving independently. Dancing with the ladies. Leaping with the lords. Swaying with the rats.

They had more life than Krampus did.

He knelt there, hands on the floor, breathing shallowly, and felt nothing. Everything was too much. The noise, the movement, the memories scattered everywhere—the evidence of what he'd lost, what he'd thrown away, what he'd locked in storage because looking at it hurt.

It should hurt now. It should devastate him. But he felt empty. Shut down.

A swan landed in front of him and looked him in the eye. "You're dissociating," it observed. "Common response to overwhelming—"

A lord landed on the swan. "—EXCELLENT PERCH—"

They tumbled away in a tangle of feathers and silk. Krampus didn't watch them go. He just stared at the unopened letter.

I miss working with you. Can we talk?

287 years. He'd left it sealed for 287 years.

The memory surfaced unbidden, sharp and

unwelcome as a blade. He remembered when it arrived. Three weeks after the final inquiry. He'd been standing in the North Pole hallway, formal disciplinary paperwork finally signed, when he saw Santa across the corridor. Not angry. Worse than angry. Weary. The look of a partner re-evaluating risk. Santa had opened his mouth, closed it, walked away. The letter had arrived that evening by courier.

Krampus had held it, felt its weight, seen his own name in Santa's familiar script. And he'd known—known with absolute certainty—that opening it would make everything final. The distance. The doubt. The crack that had formed during the Plague inquiry would become a chasm, formalized in ink, impossible to bridge.

So he'd locked it away instead. If he never opened it, he could pretend it said something else. Pretend Santa still believed in him. Pretend the partnership was just dormant, not dead.

287 years of pretending. 287 years of choosing not to know over knowing the worst.

A partridge hopped closer. "When did you decide isolation was safer than—"

An explosive egg went off between them. Purple glitter everywhere. The partridge kept talking through it. "—risk? When did you choose loneliness over—"

A dancing lady swept through, pulling the partridge into a reluctant waltz.

Krampus's hands curled against the stone.

This was too much. Not the chaos itself, though that was overwhelming. It was the life of it.

All these beings. All this movement. All this noise and color and energy and connection. All of it in his space. Demanding his attention. Demanding he engage. Demanding he be part of something.

He'd been alone for so long. Three hundred years of silence, of empty rooms, of conversations with no one. Of existing in the spaces between connection because connection meant risk, and risk meant pain, and pain meant—

His breath caught.

A hen landed on his shoulder. "*Mon ami*, you are having what we call a crisis—"

A piper walked past, still piping, somehow stepping over Krampus without breaking stride or melody. The drumming in his skull crescendoed. BOOM. BOOM. BOOM.

The maids were still pulling things from storage. A banner: "KRAMPUS & SANTA: KEEPING BALANCE SINCE 1487." A shared calendar from centuries ago, both their handwriting marking dates, making plans, coordinating. A photo of them at some celebration, arms around each other's shoulders, faces bright with genuine happiness.

Someone set it directly in front of Krampus. He looked at it. At the version of himself who knew how to be happy, who knew how to exist with others, who wasn't afraid of being part of something alive and chaotic and big.

When had he become this? This hollow thing kneeling on the floor, unable to process joy, unable to engage with chaos, unable to remember how to be anything other than alone.

"You don't know how," a dove said gently, landing near his hand. "That's why this is hard. You've been alone so long you've forgotten how to be part of something."

"—WORKPLACE DIGNITY REQUIRES—"

"—your abandonment trauma—"

"—STACK FORMATION—"

BOOM. BOOM. BOOM.

The chaos swirled. Krampus knelt.

And in the exact center of the maelstrom, Yule sat. Still purring. Still watching. Unblinking. Those amber-gold eyes fixed on Krampus with absolute focus. Not judging. Not pushing. Just watching. Waiting.

The purr cut through everything else, a constant, unwavering rumble beneath the chaos.

Krampus met the cat's eyes. Yule's pupils were wide. Dark. Bottomless.

"I can't," Krampus said. The words barely made it past his lips, swallowed by the noise. But Yule's ears twitched. He heard.

"I can't do this," Krampus said again, louder. "I don't—I've been alone too long. I don't know how to—"

How to what? How to be part of this chaos? This life? This cacophony of connection and noise and demands and presence? How to let himself be surrounded by beings who wanted things from him, who pushed and prodded and wouldn't let him hide? How to exist in a community after three centuries of isolation? How to let the walls down when they were the only thing keeping him together?

A goose honked directly in his ear. An explosive egg went off at his feet. A lord landed on his back, used him as a springboard, and leaped away shouting about trajectory. The dancing ladies tried to pull him into their formation. His body didn't move. They danced around him instead, incorporating his stillness into their choreography.

The maids kept finding memories. The partridges kept psychoanalyzing. The doves kept offering therapeutic frameworks. The hens kept unionizing. The phones kept ringing. The pipers kept piping. The drummers kept drumming in his skull.

And Krampus stayed on the floor, hands pressed to stone, unable to rise, unable to engage, unable to do anything but exist in the center of the storm and feel it all pressing down.

Too much. Too alive. Too everything.

Yule stood. He walked toward him through the chaos—lords leaping overhead, geese honking around him, rats parting to let him pass, shadows bowing. He sat down directly in front of Krampus. Face to face. Close enough that the purr vibrated through the air between them.

Those eyes. Gold and amber and ancient and knowing. Seeing everything. All of it. The fear.

The overwhelm. The three hundred years of running. The walls, the armor, the careful distance. The loneliness Krampus had convinced himself was preference.

Yule blinked slowly. Once. Didn't look away.

Around them, the chaos raged. A holiday apocalypse in full swing. Every gift active, every manifestation present, every memory exposed. Krampus's lair—his carefully controlled, perfectly isolated lair—transformed into something loud and bright and impossibly alive.

And he knelt in the center of it all, breaking apart, shutting down, drowning in the one thing he'd spent centuries avoiding: connection.

Yule purred. Watched. Waited. The chaos swirled on.

And Krampus stared into golden eyes and felt his world crack wide open.

THE NORTH POLE CALLS

A phone rang. Different from the chaos of constant ringing. This one cut through—clear, insistent, familiar.

One of the calling birds hopped to it. Pecked the answer button.

"HELLO?" a voice boomed from the speaker. Warm. Deep. Concerned. "Krampus? Are you there? We're getting reports of dimensional instability—something about exploding geese and backwards snow and—is that drumming? Why is there drumming? Krampus?"

Santa.

The calling bird looked at Krampus, still kneeling on the floor, surrounded by chaos.

Held out the phone with its beak.

Krampus stared at it.

Every instinct screamed at him to refuse. To let it ring. To maintain the distance he'd perfected over three centuries.

Santa's voice. Santa's concern. Santa who had sent a *memo* instead of standing beside him at the Tribunal. Santa who had let doubt flicker in his eyes and turned partnership into liability. Santa who had moved on while Krampus calcified into bitterness and called it principle.

Taking that phone meant breaking the pattern. Meant admitting that the isolation wasn't working. Meant risking—what? More disappointment? More evidence that he'd been right to pull away?

But.

He remembered laughing. Actually laughing, breathless and surprised, tangled in a heap of dancing ladies and leaping lords while Yule purred triumphantly on his chest. The way his face had hurt from smiling. The way something compressed in his chest had finally expanded.

He remembered Yule launching himself at hostile geese. Defending him. Choosing to protect him when no one had done that in—how long? Had anyone ever done that?

The warmth of those moments pressed against the cold of three hundred years.

The phone kept ringing in the calling bird's beak.

This was the choice. Right here. Right now. Stay isolated and safe and slowly suffocating. Or reach out and risk everything.

Around him, the maelstrom continued. Lords leaping overhead in complex aerial patterns. Dancing ladies incorporating shadows into their choreography. Geese laying explosive eggs in rhythm with the piping. Hens and partridges in heated negotiations. Maids organizing centuries of memories.

BOOM. BOOM. BOOM. The drumming in his skull.

The phone sat there, offered. Waiting.

Yule's eyes didn't leave him.

Krampus's hand moved. Reached out. Took the phone. Brought it to his ear.

The calling bird hopped away.

"Santa," Krampus said. His voice sounded hollow. Distant.

"Oh thank—what's going on? The sensors are going crazy. Half the North Pole's emergency systems just activated. Are you alright?"

A lord landed on Krampus's shoulder. Used it as a springboard. Leaped away.

An explosive egg detonated three feet to his left.

Gold glitter rained down.

A swan swam past in a puddle that definitely hadn't been there a moment ago, mid-diagnosis: "—pattern of avoidant attachment clearly manifesting in—"

"I can't do this," Krampus said.

The words came out quiet. Flat. Not angry. Not defensive. Defeated.

The chaos seemed to pause for half a second. Birds mid-flight. Lords mid-leap. Even the piping felt quieter, though it didn't actually stop.

"What?" Santa's voice shifted. Gentler. Concerned. "Krampus, what—"

"I can't do this," Krampus repeated. His hand tightened on the phone. "I don't know how to... I forgot how to be part of this."

Silence on the other end. Just Santa's breathing. The faint jingle of bells in the background.

"I know," Santa said finally. Soft. Understanding. "That's why I sent help."

Krampus's eyes went to Yule. Still sitting there. Still watching. Still purring in the center of the storm.

"This is HELP?" The word cracked. "This—all of this—this is helping?"

"You wouldn't have accepted a therapist," Santa said. Matter-of-fact. "You barely tolerate me. But you'll tolerate a cat."

A laugh escaped Krampus. Broken. Borderline hysterical.

"I've been doing this for 500 years, Santa."

"I know."

A partridge landed on the phone. Krampus didn't shake it off.

"I've been—" His throat closed. "I've been fine. I've managed. The work gets done. Everything functions."

"And you've been alone for 300 of them."

The words hit like a physical blow. Krampus's breath caught.

"That's on me," Santa continued. Quiet. Heavy with something that sounded like guilt. "I should have intervened sooner. I saw you pulling away. Saw you isolating. Told myself you needed space. That you'd reach out when you were ready."

A maid set another photo on the floor. Krampus and Santa. Laughing. Partners.

"But you weren't going to reach out," Santa said. "Were you?"

Krampus looked at the unopened letter. 287 years.

"No," he whispered.

"So I sent the cat."

The cat, who was currently purring loud enough to be heard over dimensional chaos. Who'd brought him the ornament in the middle of the night. Who'd defended him from geese. Who'd tripped him mid-dance just to make him laugh.

Who'd systematically destroyed every wall Krampus had built.

"The cat is a disaster," Krampus said.

"Yeah." Santa's voice warmed. "So were you, once. That's why we worked."

Silence.

Krampus's free hand pressed against the floor. His fingers found the edge of the photo. The one of them together. Happy. A team.

"I don't—" he started. "I don't know if I can—"

"You don't have to know," Santa interrupted gently. "You just have to let him help you."

Around them, the chaos swirled.

Partridges offering diagnoses. Doves suggesting therapeutic interventions. Hens negotiating workplace conditions. Calling birds managing a communications crisis. Geese creating explosive punctuation. Swans performing synchronized psychoanalysis. Maids organizing memories. Dancing ladies choreographing chaos. Lords leaping through it all. Pipers providing the cursed soundtrack. Drummers thundering in his skull.

And in the center: Yule.

Watching. Waiting. Those golden eyes that saw everything. That had seen him break. That had seen him laugh. That had seen him finally, after five hundred years, admit he couldn't do this alone.

Krampus looked at the cat. The cat looked back. Blinked slowly.

"Let him help you," Santa said again. Quieter. "Please."

The word hung in the air.

Please.

When was the last time Santa had said please to him? When was the last time anyone had asked instead of demanded? When was the last time someone had cared enough to intervene?

Krampus's grip on the phone tightened. His eyes stayed on Yule.

On the small god sitting calm in the storm. The chaos agent who'd been sent to break him open. The cat who'd somehow, impossibly, become his.

"Okay," Krampus whispered.

The line went dead. Not a disconnect. A completion. Santa had said what needed saying.

Now it was up to Krampus. He set the phone down.

It was immediately claimed by a calling bird, who started dialing again.

The chaos continued around him. But Krampus only saw Yule.

Yule, who stood now. Walked toward him through the maelstrom. Sat down directly in front of him. Purred.

Krampus's hand reached out. Shaking. Hovered over the cat's head. This was it. The moment. The choice.

He could pull back. Could stand up. Could try to fight this, try to regain control, try to rebuild the walls. Or he could let it happen. Could let the cat help. Could let himself be part of something alive and chaotic and terrifying and *connected*.

His hand lowered. Touched soft fur. Yule's purr intensified. Pressed his head into Krampus's palm. And something in Krampus's chest broke open completely.

Not broken like shattered. Broken like a dam releasing. Broken like spring thaw. Broken like something that had been holding too tight for too long finally, finally letting go.

His other hand came up. Both hands on the cat now. Cradling the small warm weight. The purr vibrated through his palms, up his arms, into his chest where something tight and cold had lived for three centuries.

Around them, the chaos peaked. Everything happening at once. Everything overwhelming. Everything too much. But Yule was warm. And solid. And *here*.

And for the first time in three hundred years, Krampus wasn't alone.

Chapter Seventeen

YULE'S SECRET

Yule stood. Stretched. The movement was different this time. Deliberate. Ceremonial. His front legs extended. Claws flexed. Back arched.

And the chaos *paused*. Not stopped. Paused. Like someone had pressed a button and everything froze mid-motion.

A lord hung suspended mid-leap.

A dancing lady caught mid-spin.

An explosive egg glowed but did not detonate.

The pipers' instruments were raised but silent.

The drumming in Krampus's skull stopped.

Complete. Absolute. Silence.

Yule finished his stretch. Sat down. And began to glow.

Not like the partridge's soft radiance. Not like the golden rings' warm shimmer. This was different. Ancient.

His black fur absorbed the light even as he emitted it, creating an impossible contradiction

—darkness that glowed, shadow that illuminated.

The festive sweater dissolved into light and reformed as something else. Something that looked like starlight woven into fabric, like the aurora borealis captured in thread, like every winter celebration across every century compressed into a single garment.

His eyes shifted from amber-gold to something that contained galaxies.

And when he spoke, the voice came from everywhere and nowhere, *"I am Yule."*

Not a cat's meow. Words. Old words. In a language that predated language itself but somehow Krampus understood perfectly.

"Spirit of Festive Misrule. The Chaos That Breaks Through Calcification. The Joy That Forces Its Way Back Into Rigid Systems."

The air shimmered around him. The frozen chaos began to move again—but slowly, like watching through water.

Yule's tail swished once.

Every object the cat had destroyed over the past twelve days lit up with soft light:

The locked drawer—shattered open that first day.

The filing system—scattered across the floor.

The "Professional Distance: A Manual"—sat upon, ignored, rendered meaningless.

"Every destroyed thing," Yule's voice resonated through the lair, *"was something you were hiding behind."*

The drawer glowed brighter.

"*Emotional avoidance. You kept connection locked away where it could not hurt you.*"

The scattered index cards shimmered.

"*Obsessive control. You organized suffering because you could not organize your own pain.*"

The HR manual burst into gentle flames that did not consume, just illuminated.

"*Isolation dressed as professionalism. Distance marketed as efficiency.*"

Krampus stared. His hands still hovered where Yule had been—small and warm and cat-shaped.

Now the being before him was still small, still cat-formed, but contained multitudes.

"*And every summoned creature,*" Yule continued, "*addressed something you needed to face.*"

The partridge glowed. All six of them, suspended mid-argument.

"*Purpose. When did your work stop mattering? When did duty become suffering? They asked because you had stopped asking yourself.*"

The turtle doves lit up, frozen mid-therapy session.

"*Loneliness. You needed to name it. Acknowledge it. Stop calling it preference.*"

The French hens shimmered, suspended mid-union negotiation.

"*Beauty. Joy. The things you removed from your life because efficiency felt safer than happiness.*"

The calling birds and their phones glowed with gentle light.

"Reconnection. The calls you would not make. The relationships you had severed. The isolation you maintained through silence."

The golden rings pulsed on the floor where they'd scattered.

"Memory. Who you used to be before the armor. The version of yourself who knew how to smile. How to help. How to care."

The geese—frozen mid-honk, mid-explosion—illuminated.

"Accepting protection. Accepting help. Learning that others could defend you, fight for you, care for you."

The swans glowed in their puddles, their bathtub, every water source they had claimed.

"Truth. The root cause. You were not angry at Santa. You were angry at yourself for stopping. For giving up. For choosing emptiness over risk."

The maids lit up, their hands full of memories they had pulled from storage.

"Buried history. The evidence that you were happy once. That connection was possible. That the past was not always painful."

The dancing ladies spun slowly in their frozen choreography, glowing like stars.

"Fun. Pure, simple, uncomplicated joy. Laughter for no reason except that something was absurd and wonderful."

The lords hung suspended mid-leap, each one shimmering.

"Chaos acceptance. Letting go of control. Learning to exist in disorder without fighting it."

The pipers and their instruments pulsed with light.

"Endurance through discomfort. Staying present when everything felt wrong. Not running. Not hiding. Just... staying."

And finally, the drummers—invisible but present, their rhythm still echoing in the silence.

"Facing everything at once. No more avoiding. No more compartmentalizing. Every fear, every pain, every truth, all together."

The lights pulsed in sequence. Each day. Each gift. Each perfectly targeted intervention.

Krampus's breath came shallow.

"It was not random," he said. Not a question. A realization.

"No," Yule confirmed. *"It was therapy disguised as catastrophe."*

"You—" Krampus looked at the glowing being before him. "You broke me."

"I broke the walls. You were already breaking underneath them."

The chaos began moving again. Faster now. The partridges resumed their argument. The doves circled. The hens negotiated. The calls connected. The rings glowed. The geese exploded. The swans psychoanalyzed. The maids organized. The ladies danced. The lords leaped. The pipers piped.

But Krampus understood now. Saw the pattern.

Each day had not been random misfortune. Each manifestation had not been cosmic coincidence. It had been surgical. Precise. Targeted.

Every single moment designed to crack through three hundred years of carefully constructed isolation.

"You knew," Krampus said. "From the beginning. You knew exactly what you were doing."

"I am Misrule," Yule said simply. *"I know where joy is trapped. I know what is keeping it there. I know how to break it free."*

"By destroying everything."

"By destroying the cages. The joy was always yours. You just forgot where you put it."

The light around Yule intensified. The chaos swirled faster—all twelve days active, all twelve lessons present, all twelve interventions working in concert.

And Krampus knelt in the center of it all, finally understanding.

The cat had not been random. The chaos had not been punishment. It had been precision. Every knocked-over lamp. Every destroyed filing system. Every explosive goose and psychoanalyzing swan and union-negotiating hen. All of it carefully calculated to reach the parts of him he had buried so deep he had forgotten they existed.

"The question," Yule said, his form beginning to shift again, galaxies in his eyes dimming back

to amber-gold, starlight fading to black fur, *"is what you do now."*

The glow receded. The ancient presence compressed back into cat shape. The festive sweater reappeared.

And Yule sat there—small and fluffy and purring—like he had not just revealed himself as an ancient spirit of cosmic chaos.

Krampus stared.

Around them, the twelve days of chaos continued their synchronized catastrophe. Every destroyed thing visible. Every lesson active. Every truth exposed.

His lair was falling apart. *He* was falling apart. But now he knew why. And knowing changed everything.

"What do I do now?" Krampus repeated quietly.

Yule purred. Blinked slowly.

Ask for help, the purr seemed to say.

Let it happen.

Choose connection over control.

The chaos peaked around them. Everything converging. Everything exposed. Everything breaking open.

And Krampus knelt there, hands still extended where the cat had been, understanding finally settling into his bones:

This was not happening *to* him. It was happening *for* him. All of it.

The question was whether he would let it finish.

Chapter Eighteen

THE CHOICE

The chaos raged on.

Yule sat in his cat form, purring, watching. Waiting.

Everything was still happening. Partridges arguing. Doves circling. Hens negotiating. Phones ringing. Geese exploding. Swans analyzing. Maids organizing. Ladies dancing. Lords leaping. Pipers piping.

The drumming had resumed in Krampus's skull. *BOOM. BOOM. BOOM.*

The dimensional instability was getting worse. Reality bent at the edges. The walls shimmered. The floor felt uncertain.

His lair was tearing itself apart. And Yule just sat there. Purring. Calm. Like he was waiting for something.

"Stop it," Krampus said.

Yule's ear twitched. But the chaos continued.

A lord landed on Krampus's head. An explosive egg detonated by his knee. A swan tried to initiate emergency psychoanalysis. A dancing lady pulled him halfway into a reluctant spin before the partridge interrupted with observations about avoidant coping mechanisms.

"STOP IT," Krampus said louder.

Yule blinked slowly. The chaos didn't stop.

The Spirit of Festive Misrule—ancient, powerful, capable of bending reality—sat there in cat form and did nothing. Because he was waiting.

The realization hit like cold water. Yule could stop this. Could end it with a thought. Could pull all twelve days back, restore order, make everything go away. But he wouldn't. Not unless—

Krampus's throat closed.

Around him, the storm raged. Lords ricocheting off every surface. Geese laying explosive eggs in rapid succession. Maids pulling more and more memories from storage—photos, letters, decorations, evidence of everything he'd lost.

All that noise. All that movement. All that *connection* he'd been running from. Three hundred years of running. And now Yule was asking him to stop. Was asking him to turn around and face it. Was asking him to—

His hands clenched.

Ask for help.

The words formed in his mind but stuck in his throat. He didn't ask for help. Didn't need it. Didn't want it. Had managed alone for centuries and could keep managing alone because that was safer and easier and less painful than admitting—

An explosive egg went off directly at his feet. Pink glitter coated his legs. A shadow-dancer pirouetted through him. The piping drilled into his skull.

BOOM. BOOM. BOOM.

He couldn't do this alone.

He *couldn't*.

The admission formed like a stone in his chest. Heavy. Solid. Undeniable. He couldn't keep going like this. Couldn't rebuild the walls. Couldn't go back to the silence and the cold coffee and the empty lair and the work that felt like grinding obligation instead of purpose.

He couldn't. But asking—

Asking meant admitting weakness. Admitting failure. Admitting that three hundred years of isolation had been a mistake. Admitting that he needed something. Needed *someone*.

Admitting he couldn't do this alone.

The chaos swirled. Yule sat. Waited.

Those amber eyes that had seen everything. That had witnessed every moment of the past twelve days. That had watched him break and laugh and dance and finally, finally crack open.

That had brought him the ornament in the middle of the night when he couldn't sleep. That had defended him from hostile geese. That had tripped him mid-waltz just to hear him laugh. That had sat on his chest and purred until he fell asleep for the first time in years. That had systematically destroyed every defense he'd built and then sat patiently waiting for him to be ready.

Krampus looked at the small cat in the center of the storm.

All those creatures. All that noise. All that connection screaming at him from every direction. Everything he'd avoided. Everything he'd feared. Everything he'd convinced himself he didn't need.

His knees hit the floor. He knelt down to cat level. Face to face with the Spirit of Festive Misrule wearing a ridiculous holiday sweater.

The chaos raged around them. Lords leaping. Ladies spinning. Geese exploding. Maids organizing. Every manifestation active, demanding, overwhelming.

And Yule sat there. Waiting.

For him to ask. If he didn't—

The thought crystallized with startling clarity.

If he didn't ask, the chaos would stop. Yule would end it himself, eventually. Would dispel the manifestations, seal the dimensional tears, restore order.

And then he would leave.

The thought hit like a physical blow. Yule would leave. The lair would be empty again. Silent again. Just Krampus and his filing cabinets and his cold coffee and the crushing weight of centuries pressing down with no purr to soften it, no warm weight in his lap, no one to bring him ornaments in the middle of the night or trip him mid-dance just to hear him laugh.

He'd be alone again.

And somehow—impossibly, terrifyingly—that future was worse than the chaos surrounding him now.

He looked at Yule. Really looked. Not at the Spirit of Festive Misrule. Not at the chaos agent sent by Santa. At the cat who had defended him from hostile geese, putting himself between Krampus and danger without hesitation. The cat who had brought him the ornament—K & S— when he couldn't sleep, carrying it carefully in his mouth like an offering. The one who had purred on his chest every night since, a warm solid weight that made the silence bearable. The furry black creature who had tripped him during the dance, not out of malice, but to force joy past his defenses. The feline who had systematically destroyed every wall he'd built, not to hurt him, but to *free* him.

He's been trying to help all along.

The realization settled like a key turning in a lock. Not chaos for chaos's sake. Care disguised as catastrophe. Precision wrapped in fur and festive sweaters. Every destroyed thing. Every summoned creature. Every moment of overwhelming noise and color and life.

All of it designed to break through. To reach him. To help. But only if he asked.

His throat worked. The word was right there. One syllable. Simple. Impossible.

Please.

He knew what it would cost. Three hundred years of pride. Of telling himself he didn't need anyone, couldn't need anyone, wouldn't survive needing anyone. Of building armor so thick he'd forgotten what his own skin felt like. Of substituting control for connection and calling it strength.

All of it would burn away with that one word. Every carefully constructed defense. Every wall. Every piece of distance he'd put between himself and the world. Gone.

If he said it, he would be completely exposed. Vulnerable. At the mercy of a universe that had already hurt him once, badly enough that he'd spent three centuries running from the wound.

Please meant surrendering everything he'd used to keep himself safe.

His hands trembled. But.

But.

He looked around at the chaos. At the memories scattered across his floor. At the photo of him and Santa, laughing. At the unopened letter he'd hidden from for two hundred and eighty-seven years. At the ornament that represented everything he'd lost.

At the evidence of three hundred years spent slowly suffocating while telling himself he was fine.

At the proof that he'd been dying by inches in his carefully maintained isolation. The cost of asking was high. But the cost of staying alone—

That cost was higher. Had always been higher. He'd just been too afraid to admit it.

His breath shuddered out.

If I don't ask, I lose him. I lose all of this. I go back to the silence and the cold and the empty chair and the locked drawers and the conviction that this is what I deserve.

If I do ask, I lose my armor. But maybe—maybe I gain something worth more than protection.

Maybe I gain a life.

The choice crystallized. Stay safe and alone. Or risk everything for connection. Three hundred years of one. Twelve days of the other.

And he knew—*knew* with bone-deep certainty—which one had made him feel alive.

The words formed. Stuck. His throat worked. Nothing came out.

The chaos peaked around them. A lord crashed into a dancing lady who fell into a swan who splashed a maid who dropped a box of photos that scattered across the floor—all of them showing Krampus smiling. Happy. Connected. *Alive.*

He looked at those photos. At the evidence of who he used to be. The version of himself who knew how to ask for help because he knew he deserved it. His mouth opened.

"I don't want to do this alone anymore."

The words came out quiet. Broken. But they came out.

Yule's eyes widened slightly. The purr intensified. But he didn't move. Didn't act. Still waiting. Because saying it wasn't enough. Admitting it wasn't enough. He had to *ask*.

Had to make himself vulnerable. Had to reach out. Had to actually, explicitly request help from another being after three centuries of refusing it. Had to say the word he hadn't said—hadn't *meant*—in longer than he could remember.

Krampus's hands were shaking. He lowered his head. Eye level with a cat. With an ancient spirit who'd broken him open and was now waiting—patiently, endlessly—for him to take the final step.

His throat closed completely. His chest felt like it was caving in. The word sat there. Right there. One syllable that would cost him everything. Every wall. Every defense. Every carefully constructed piece of armor he'd built to keep himself safe.

All of it would fall away with one word. One simple word. One impossible word.

The chaos raged. Yule waited.

And Krampus knelt on his floor, surrounded by the wreckage of his isolation, and forced his mouth to form the shape of surrender:

"Please."

The word came out barely louder than a breath. But it came out.

"Please," he said again, louder. "Please help me. I can't—I don't—"

His voice broke. "Please."

The word cost him everything. Every wall crumbled. Every defense shattered. Every piece of armor he'd spent three hundred years building fell away in an instant.

He was completely exposed. Completely vulnerable. Completely, utterly defenseless.

And Yule moved. Stepped forward. Pressed his small warm head against Krampus's hand. Rubbed. Hard. Purring so loud it drowned out the piping, the drumming, the chaos. His whole body pressed into the touch. Leaning. Trusting. Accepting.

I'm here, the gesture said.

I've always been here.

You just had to ask.

Krampus's other hand came up. Both hands on the cat now. Cradling the small warm weight like it was the only solid thing in a tilting world. His forehead lowered. Pressed against Yule's head. And something in his chest broke open completely. Not the crack from before. Not the slow thaw. A complete rupture.

Three hundred years of held breath released all at once. Tears he didn't know he had burned behind his eyes. His hands shook. His breath came ragged. And Yule just pressed closer. Purred louder. Solid and warm and *here.*

"I can't do this alone," Krampus whispered into soft fur. "I tried. I can't."

Yule's purr intensified.

"I need—" The words stuck again. "I need help. I need—"

Connection. Community. Joy. Purpose. Meaning.

Someone to care. Someone to help. Someone to just be here.

All of it. Everything he'd denied himself. Everything he'd locked away. Everything he'd convinced himself he didn't deserve.

"I need you," Krampus said finally. Simply. "All of you. The chaos and the noise and the connection and the—I need it. I need—"

His voice broke completely.

Yule headbutted him gently.

I know, the gesture said.

I've always known.

That's why I came.

Around them, the chaos began to shift. Still present. Still active. But changing. Waiting. Because Krampus had asked. Had admitted he needed help. Had finally, after three hundred years, reached out.

And Yule had answered. Was here. Would help. Was already helping just by being solid and warm and purring against his hands.

Krampus knelt there, holding a cat, tears threatening to fall, every defense stripped away, completely vulnerable for the first time in centuries.

And it was terrifying. And it was necessary. And it was, somehow, the first step toward something that might eventually feel like healing.

Yule purred. The chaos waited. And Krampus held on.

Chapter Nineteen

THE BARGAIN

Yule pulled back from Krampus's hands. Stood. The air around him shimmered.

The chaos began to respond—the piping quieting, the drumming fading, the dimensional tears starting to seal.

Then Yule paused. Sat down. Stared at Krampus with those ancient amber eyes.

The chaos paused with him. Half-dispelled. The pipers' instruments lowering but not fully silent. The lords mid-descent from their leaps. The dimensional resonance humming but not resolved. Waiting.

Krampus wiped his face. "What?"

Yule's tail swished once.

There will be terms, the gesture said clearly.

"Terms."

Yule's eyes narrowed slightly. Not angry. Negotiating. A meow. Pointed. Deliberate.

Then he stood, walked to the corner where the maids had stacked supplies, and sat down next to a cat bed. The fancy heated kind that Krampus definitely didn't own. Meowed again.

"A heated bed," Krampus said slowly. "You want a heated bed."

Yule's tail swished in confirmation.

"That's... reasonable."

Yule walked to the kitchen. Sat by the counter. Meowed twelve times in rapid succession.

"Twelve treats. Daily."

Another tail swish.

Krampus's mouth twitched. "That's excessive."

Yule stared.

"But fine."

Yule padded to the desk. Sat down next to the ornament—K & S intertwined—and very deliberately put his paw on it.

"Unlimited ornament rights," Krampus said. His chest tightened. "You want unlimited ornament rights."

Yule's paw pressed down gently. Possessively.

Not just this ornament. All of them. The ones the maids had pulled from storage. The evidence of celebration, of joy, of connection. Permission to keep them out. To display them. To make them part of the lair instead of locked away where they couldn't hurt.

"That's..." Krampus's throat closed. "Concerning."

Yule meowed.

Non-negotiable, the sound said.

"Fine."

But Yule wasn't done. He walked to a box of decorations. Sat down. Stared at Krampus. Meowed.

"You want me to keep them up," Krampus said quietly. "The decorations. Not just out. Up."

Yule's slow blink confirmed it.

No more locking joy away. No more bare walls. No more stripping the lair of anything that might suggest warmth or life or connection.

The decorations stayed.

Krampus's hands clenched. "Okay."

Yule walked to the phone. The one where Santa had called. Sat down next to it. Meowed once. Long. Pointed.

"No," Krampus said immediately.

Yule's stare intensified.

"Absolutely not."

The cat didn't blink. Didn't look away.

"Once a year," Krampus said. "You want me to visit Santa once a year. Minimum."

Yule's tail swished.

Yes.

"That's not—I don't need to—we have quarterly reviews—"

Yule meowed. Louder. Not a review. Not a formal check-in. Not a professional obligation.

A *visit*. Like they used to. Like partners. Like friends. Like the version of them in all those photos scattered across the floor, arms around each other's shoulders, laughing.

Krampus looked at the phone. At the evidence of three hundred years of distance that had started with good intentions and ended with complete isolation.

"Fine," he whispered. "Once a year."

But Yule still wasn't done. He walked back to Krampus. Sat directly in front of him. Eye level, because Krampus was still kneeling on the floor. Stared. Meowed.

The sound was different this time. Not a demand. A question.

The final term, it said. *The one that matters most.*

Krampus waited.

Yule's eyes didn't waver.

The lair held its breath. The half-dispelled chaos frozen mid-resolution. Lords suspended. Ladies paused. Geese quiet. Even the rats stopped swaying.

The entire holiday dimension waiting.

"What?" Krampus asked.

Yule leaned forward. Touched his nose to Krampus's hand. Pulled back. Meowed again.

And somehow, impossibly, Krampus understood exactly what was being asked.

"That last one wasn't part of the—"

Yule's stare intensified. Unblinking. Unwavering. Absolutely, completely serious.

The silence stretched. Krampus's throat worked.

This was it. The final admission. The one he'd been avoiding for three centuries. Saying he didn't want to be alone was one thing. Admitting he wasn't *fine* being alone was something else entirely.

One was a preference. A choice he could change. The other was a confession. A truth he'd been denying. An acknowledgment that he'd been lying to himself for so long he'd almost believed it.

His mouth opened. Closed.

Yule waited. The chaos waited. The entire dimension held its breath.

Krampus looked at the cat. At the Spirit of Festive Misrule who'd broken him open and put him back together and was now demanding— not asking, *demanding*—that he speak the final truth.

"...I'm not fine being alone."

The words came out barely louder than a whisper. But they came out.

Yule's eyes narrowed slightly.

All of it.

Krampus's hands clenched.

"I haven't been fine for a long time."

His voice cracked on the last word. The admission hung in the air. Raw. Honest. The final piece of armor falling away.

He wasn't fine. Hadn't been fine. Had been slowly suffocating in isolation while telling himself it was preference, was choice, was what he wanted.

Had been dying by inches for three hundred years and calling it efficiency.

"I'm not fine," he said again. Louder. "I haven't been fine. I've been—"

Miserable. Lonely. Empty. Running on resentment and obligation and the fading memory of when work had felt like purpose.

"I've been barely existing," he finished quietly. "And calling it living."

Yule purred. Loud. Immediate. Satisfied.

Good, the purr said. *Truth.*

Then he stood. Stretched. And the chaos began to dispel. For real this time.

The shimmer in the air intensified. The dimensional tears sealed. The resonance that had held everything in suspended catastrophe began to unwind.

The pipers lowered their instruments completely. Silent at last. They turned, bowed in unison to Krampus, and dissolved into light.

The drumming in his skull stopped. Just... stopped. The relief was immediate and overwhelming. Silence rushed in where the constant *BOOM BOOM BOOM* had been.

The lords descended from their final leaps. Landed gracefully. One by one they approached Krampus, each bowing with exaggerated flourish.

"Excellent perch," one said seriously.

"Adequate trajectory," another agreed.

"For a peasant," a third added.

Then they vanished in a cascade of silk and arrogance.

The dancing ladies finished their

choreography with a final, perfect spin. They curtsied—to Krampus, to Yule, to the chaos they'd incorporated into art—and dissolved into music that faded on the air.

The swans swam a final synchronized pattern in the bathtub. Rose from the water. Regarded Krampus with knowing eyes.

"Follow-up session in three months," the first one said.

"We'll be checking in," the second confirmed.

"This isn't over," the third added. Not a threat. A promise.

They lifted into flight and disappeared through the ceiling.

The maids finished their final organization. Every surface clean. Every memory visible but carefully displayed. The storage room reorganized. The lair transformed from austere functionality into something that looked *lived in*.

One maid approached with a clipboard.

"Maintenance schedule," she said, handing it to him. "Dust weekly. Don't lock things away again. Keep the windows open."

"I don't have windows."

"You will by morning." She smiled. "We took the liberty."

They vanished in a shimmer of efficient magic.

The geese waddled over in formation. The meanest one—the one Yule had befriended—honked once. Not aggressive. Almost... fond.

It laid an egg at Krampus's feet. Normal. Non-explosive. A gift.

Then the geese turned and waddled through a portal that opened to somewhere green and warm and safe.

The calling birds disconnected their final calls:

"Loki says good luck."

"Derek hopes you have a nice day."

"Brenda wants you to know her pot roast recipe is in the mail."

They chirped once in unison and disappeared.

The golden rings rose from where they'd scattered. Floated in a circle around Krampus and Yule. Glowed once—bright and warm—then dissolved into light that settled over everything like a blessing.

The French hens descended from their perch. Vivienne hopped forward with a document in her beak. She set it on the desk.

"Our contract," she said. "*Signed and ratified.* You have agreed to maintain beauty, dignity, and joy in this workplace. We will be monitoring compliance."

"*Avec plaisir,*" Colette added.

"*Bonne chance, mon ami,*" Brigitte finished.

They vanished in a flurry of elegant feathers.

The turtle doves landed on Krampus's shoulders. One on each side.

"You did well," the first said softly.

"This was hard," the second added. "But necessary."

"Keep going," they said together.

They nuzzled against his horns once. Then flew away.

The partridge—the very first manifestation, the one who'd asked when he last enjoyed his work—hopped down from the pear tree.

Regarded Krampus with those knowing eyes.

"Better," it said simply.

Then it did something unexpected. Saluted. One wing raised. Crisp. Military precise. But the eyes were warm.

"You're going to be okay," the partridge said.

Then it was gone.

The rats dispersed. The shadows returned to their proper places—still moving independently but no longer crowding. The pear tree remained, but settled, its roots somehow integrated into the stone floor like it had always been there.

One by one, the manifestations faded. The chaos dispelled. The catastrophe resolved. But the *warmth* remained.

The decorations stayed up. The photos on the walls. The ornament on the desk. The organized memories. The cleaned surfaces. The furniture the maids had somehow repaired or replaced. The guest chair that didn't gather dust anymore.

The windows that would appear by morning. The union contract signed by French hens. The maintenance schedule. The follow-up session scheduled with swans.

The evidence everywhere that he wasn't alone anymore. That connection had been forced back into his life and had left permanent marks. Good marks.

The silence settled. Real silence this time. Not oppressive. Not empty. Just... quiet.

Krampus knelt on his floor, surrounded by the aftermath of twelve days of surgical chaos, and breathed.

Yule walked over. Rubbed against his hand. Purred.

Krampus's fingers sank into soft fur.

"Your terms are excessive," he said quietly.

Yule purred louder.

"And manipulative."

The purr intensified.

"And I agreed to all of them."

Yule slow-blinked.

Yes, the gesture said. *You did.*

Krampus looked around his transformed lair. At the decorations. The photos. The memories. The evidence that joy had lived here once and could live here again. At the warmth that remained even though the chaos had gone.

"Thank you," he whispered.

Yule headbutted his hand.

You're welcome.

Now get me those twelve treats.

Despite everything—the emotional devastation, the admissions, the tears threatening behind his eyes—Krampus laughed. Quietly. But genuinely.

And Yule purred, and the lair was warm, and somewhere in the distance a phone rang that Krampus knew he'd actually answer this time.

The lair was still dark.

Stone walls. Cold floors. The architecture of someone who'd chosen function over comfort for five centuries. Fundamentally, it was still *his*.

But there were decorations now. Garland draped along the mantle—not excessively, just enough to soften the austere lines. A string of bells hung by the door, chiming softly when the wind came through the new windows. The maids had been right. He'd woken up to find them there —actual windows, with actual light, showing the alpine landscape he'd been living in without seeing for decades.

The pear tree still grew through what used to be his dining table. The maids had built around it. Now it was a feature, not a disaster. Someone (probably Vivienne) had hung ornaments on it.

The old ornament—K & S intertwined—sat in a place of prominence on the highest branch. Visible from everywhere in the main room.

Below it: newer additions. A small carved cat. Another that looked suspiciously like a goose. One shaped like a tiny sweater. And several that

Krampus definitely hadn't put there but that made him almost-smile every time he saw them.

Yule was currently in the corner, wearing today's sweater—this one green with gold bells that actually jingled when he moved—absolutely destroying a ball of enchanted yarn.

The yarn fought back. Defended itself. Tried to tie him up. Yule won every time.

He pounced, rolled, kicked with his back legs, emerged victorious with yarn in his teeth, then attacked again.

The picture of noble dignity in festive knitwear.

Krampus's filing system was still there. Floor-to-ceiling cabinets. Color-coded. Cross-referenced. Meticulously organized by region and severity.

But on top of the main cabinet: a heated cat bed. Expensive. Plush. With a small pillow embroidered with a "Y." Yule's bed, from the bargain. He never used it.

Preferred laps. Or shoulders. Or the middle of Krampus's desk. Or anywhere that wasn't the bed specifically purchased for him. But it stayed there anyway.

Below it, the files were exactly as organized as they'd always been. Except for the paw prints. Small. Deliberate. On random folders throughout the system. Evidence that Yule walked across them regularly, inspecting Krampus's work, leaving his mark.

Krampus didn't mind. Couldn't bring himself

to mind. The prints were proof of presence. Of company. Of chaos integrated into order instead of destroying it.

A knock at the door.

Krampus looked up.

Deliveries were rare. Visitors rarer.

He opened the door to find a card. Red envelope. North Pole postage.

Inside, Santa's handwriting:

Thank you for participating in the Goodwill Outreach Initiative. Your cooperation is appreciated.

—S.C.

P.S. Heard it went well. Knew it would.

Below that, attached with a paperclip: a coupon.

GOOD FOR: One (1) Additional Cat
No Expiration Date

Krampus stared at it.

"Absolutely not," he said aloud.

From across the room, Yule's purr changed. Took on a quality that sounded distinctly smug.

Distinctly like *we'll see about that.*

Krampus looked over to find the cat watching him, yarn forgotten, eyes gleaming with something that might have been mischief or might have been ancient cosmic knowledge. Probably both.

"No," Krampus repeated. "No second cat. Never. Not happening."

Yule's purr intensified.

That night, Krampus found a pamphlet on his pillow.

Alpine Kitten Adoption: Finding Forever Homes for Magical Felines

He crumpled it up. Threw it away. Found it back on his pillow the next morning, carefully smoothed out. Threw it away again. It returned. Eventually he gave up and shoved it in a drawer. Where it would stay. Definitely.

The work continued.

The naughty list didn't maintain itself. Children kept making poor choices that required documentation and appropriate consequences.

Krampus sat at his desk, updating files, preparing for the season. But Yule was on his lap. Had been for the past hour. Purring steadily. Making typing difficult. Occasionally batting at the pen when Krampus tried to write notes. Making work slower. Less efficient. Better.

A flutter of wings. The partridge landed on

the pear tree branch, the one it had claimed as its own.

"You're using passive voice again," it observed, peering at Krampus's notes. "Weakens the impact of corrective feedback."

"It's fine."

"Is it, though?"

Krampus sighed. Made the edit.

"Better," the partridge said. "Also, when did you last take a break? You've been working for three hours."

"I'm fine."

"Are you? Or are you falling into old patterns of using work to avoid—"

"I'll take a break in twenty minutes."

"Hmm." The partridge settled onto its branch. "I'll hold you to that."

It would. It came by twice a week now. Offered critiques. Asked pointed questions. Refused to let Krampus backslide into isolation disguised as productivity.

He'd started listening.

From down the hall, sounds of activity.

Vivienne had moved in. Not permanently—the hens had their own space somewhere verdant and French and full of whatever aesthetic beauty they demanded. But she kept a room here. "For monitoring workplace compliance," she'd said.

Really, she just liked company. Liked conversation. Liked making sure Krampus ate meals that weren't cold coffee and resentment.

Last week she'd made coq au vin. It had been delicious. He hadn't told her that. She knew anyway.

On the door—the main door, the one that led from his private quarters to the outside world—hung a small wreath. Simple. Evergreen. A red ribbon. Nothing excessive. Nothing that screamed celebration. Just... acknowledgment.

That this was a home now. Not just a workspace. That someone lived here. And visitors were, occasionally, welcome.

Krampus glanced at the window.

Snow was falling. Downward. The correct direction. White flakes drifting past the glass, covering the Alps in fresh powder. Normal. Natural. Non-magical.

The dimensional chaos had resolved completely. Reality had settled back into its proper configuration. With some permanent adjustments.

He was still grumpy. Scowled at his files. Muttered when Yule knocked his pen off the desk for the third time. Grumbled when the partridge offered yet another psychological assessment disguised as literary criticism. But he wasn't alone anymore.

The lair was full. Of decorations. Of memories on walls. Of a pear tree. Of a cat in his lap. Of a partridge in residence. Of a French hen down the hall. Of evidence everywhere that life had been forcibly reintroduced and had decided to stay.

His filing system had a note stuck to it. Pink. Probably from Vivienne.

> Brunch with Santa - Sunday -
> 11 AM
> Don't forget!!

Krampus had circled it. In red pen. Added a note in his own handwriting: *Bring the contract. Discuss quarterly review process.*

Because he couldn't just have brunch. Had to make it partly professional. Had to maintain some distance. But he'd circled it. Had put it on his calendar. Had every intention of going.

The first visit in 287 years. Part of the bargain. Part of the healing.

Yule shifted in his lap, stretched, yawned. His paw reached out. Deliberately pushed Krampus's coffee mug toward the edge of the desk.

"Don't," Krampus said.

Yule's paw pressed further. The mug teetered.

"Yule."

The paw gave one final push. The mug went over. Hit the floor. Didn't shatter—it was the new one, ceramic, sturdy enough to survive a cat. Coffee spread across the stone.

Krampus looked at the mess. At Yule, sitting in his lap, utterly unrepentant. At the decorations on the walls. The memories displayed. The evidence that chaos had been invited in and had transformed everything.

"Every single day with you," he said.

Yule purred. Pressed his head into Krampus's hand. Demanding attention. Demanding affection. Demanding that Krampus stop working for five minutes and acknowledge the small warm creature in his lap who'd saved his life by destroying it first.

Krampus's hand moved. Scratched behind Yule's ears. Found the spot that made the purr intensify to ridiculous levels. His other hand stayed on the file. Maintaining the pretense of working.

But his attention was on the cat. On the wreath on the door. On the circled note about Sunday brunch. On the partridge dozing in the pear tree.On the sounds of Vivienne singing something in French down the hall.On the warmth that filled his lair now. That seeped into the cold stones and the dark corners and the places that had been empty for so long they'd forgotten what full felt like.

Yule purred.

The snow fell.

The decorations caught the light.

And Krampus sat at his desk—still working, still grumpy, still fundamentally himself. And maybe, just maybe—he smiled.

ABOUT THE AUTHOR

Kysa Steele is an IT professional by day, and by night an author, TTRPG GM, cat servant, and wife (though the order depends on which cat is asking). She grew up devouring books and plotting to write her own. While newly minted as an indie author, she's been telling elaborate, occasionally cursed stories at the TTRPG table for years.

Her cat-centric fiction spans dark fantasy, detective noir, portal adventures, and apocalyptic comedy. The Infurnal Catastrophe series features a cursed demon princess and infernal magic, while the Orange Protocol follows a hard-boiled detective trapped in a cat's body and scattered across a psychic network of orange tabbies. Her Unfamiliar Territory series stars Mischief, a portal-hopping cat whose curiosity threatens entire dimensions. She spends her time building worlds and trying to unravel her cats' many conspiracies.

She lives in Texas with her husband and a cadre of furry overlords. Nori and Mochi are the latest recruits, while Nox, nicknamed the Demon

Princess, claimed dominion during the writing of Curse Meow Not. Jake Speed and his sister Ripley occupy the middle ranks, and the eldest, Cid, remains her watchful shadow and self-appointed bodyguard.

ALSO BY KYSA STEELE

Curse Meow Not

Velzara was forged for the apocalypse—destined to burn worlds. Now she's a fluffy black housecat adopted by a young witch who thinks "Nox" is just a stray with attitude problems. But when ancient curses start rearranging the walls and something far more dangerous than a fallen demon princess is lurking in the house, Velzara faces an impossible choice: reclaim her monstrous birthright or protect the mortal girl who's starting to feel like home.

Containment Not Recommended

Luis Cannon was a hardboiled detective until the Cognichonk shattered his consciousness across a psychic network of orange cats. When they sync, they solve mysteries with noir narration. When the signal fades, they scream at ceiling fans. But something's wrong—cats are going lucid, occult sigils are spreading like magical malware, and the Cognichonk is choosing sides.

Cat Out of Luck

Mischief just wanted to jazz up a boring ritual, nap, and maybe snag a few sardines for later. Instead, he

got trapped in a human body and discovered
something is hunting familiars across dimensions,
harvesting them as magical batteries. The universe
made a terrible mistake giving him any responsibility.
He's going to make it everyone's problem.